Martha Everts Holden

Amber Glints

Martha Everts Holden

Amber Glints

ISBN/EAN: 9783742812483

Manufactured in Europe, USA, Canada, Australia, Japa

Cover: Foto ©Andreas Hilbeck / pixelio.de

Manufactured and distributed by brebook publishing software
(www.brebook.com)

Martha Everts Holden

Amber Glints

Amber Glints

By Amber,

Author of "Rosemary and Rue."

Chicago and New York:
Rand, McNally & Company.

Copyright, 1897, by W. W. Denslow.

INTRODUCTION.

Where she was born, or when, are matters of no consequence at all. Regarding her, the event is when you met her. The incidents are the subsequent meetings,—with occasional pictures she brings you of the pleasures or the miseries of some day that intervened. I have immensely enjoyed her tribulations. There is something so ideally complete about them; their agony is so absolutely perfect, so hopeless and utter, and so infallibly eternal, that they are very satisfying. And her joys are just as artistic. I don't think much of snow storms myself, but the description of one which she brought me filled my ears with that musical silence of a winter night, stirred my blood with the tonic of frost, and filled my soul with marvel at the grandeur she had caught. Hot days do not delight me. But when she has come in with the blaze of midsummer fairly glorifying her, fusing the little things of life into greatness, melting conventionality, consuming pride, I have been thankful one Gheber is left me.

I have never known quite so finely strung an organism. Her possibilities are almost infinite. Her appreciation of noble things may not prove her ability any more than her singularly accurate conceptions of infamy prove her bad. But her actions prove her noble beyond the limits of most women. Her permanent residence is on a height, close to the beauties we can dimly see; and her mission is to transcribe the laws of that later Sinai for us who dwell in the valleys—trying with small success to leave all golden calves unworshiped. Her constant progress is along a pathway on the sword-sharp sierra which divides the world; and all the kingdoms of the earth with their fullness is on the right, and all the abject suffering is on the left. And both are hers. How she would take from plenty for the banishment of penury if she could, we that know her can well understand. How she daily perils her already narrow footing by supplying her left hand before her right is full we also know—and we have laughed at her toppling struggles many a time.

Amber is a Bohemian of Bohemia. She doesn't fit convention. She despises it. One wonders she did not enter into her kingdom long ago. The quick wit that springs spontaneous from the soul of surprise is as old wine to her! The stilted humor that comes in the evening dress of prepared occasions is as last night's lees. Piping songs contain no music; but the resonance and breadth and depth that roll from power's organ are her anthems.

And yet the woman is an aristocrat. She has no patience with socialism, and no mercy for anarchists. She loves jewels—and wears them, to her heart's delight. When law was strangled here in Chicago a year ago; when commerce was writhing under feet of men who did not know the blessedness of industry; when the badge of civilization's enmity was a white ribbon—and weak men and women were wearing it for self-protection, she came up in the elevator with a group of labeled serfs, cried out upon them, and said she would rather ride with smallpox patients. It made her enemies for a day. And in that day she was almost happy. But no drop of a sycophant's blood troubles her veins. As miserable a night as she ever passed was that in the drawing-room of a great lady who wanted to cultivate her, if she had known how—and had dared; and poor Amber, almost worshiped by thousands, was as the most embarrassed cypher when she came to make her adieu. It was not her atmosphere.

Bohemia is; and there she reigns. It was her own creation. She invited two or three people for an evening weekly, and the room grew quickly too small for those who came. Bohemia moved its frontiers, and now, after much migration, the tribe has a local habitation. Perhaps a hundred persons come to the weekly meetings. The work is to keep away aliens. Those to the manner born either can do good things, or they know when good things are done. It is there the tenors whose stage songs are superb, breathe the air of their home, touch hand with their brothers, and sing divinely. It is there the raconteur, whose characters walk in procession where riches and conventionality pay, himself becomes those characters, and we laugh—not at them, but with them. The music there is not for sale. The eloquence may not be purchased. The good-fellowship is beyond all price. And from first to last Amber is Queen of Bohemia.

What has she done? Well she has written tomes of the most beautiful poetry—with and without rhyme—which has glorified Chicago newspapers. She has reached a myriad of men and women who know her name, who thank her because of her message; who love her because of the soul that she coins into "jeweled odes, and epigrams just five words long;" who are helped by her philosophies; who are chastened by her lectures; who are comforted as angels might comfort by the rhythmic beauty of her lines. I do not believe there is a writer in the country who has touched with so strong a personal influence so many readers; who has so wonderfully attached to her so numerous and so sensibly interested an audience. I really do not believe any other writer has comforted so many in trouble, has added color to the delight of so many who were happy, has led into light so many who were confused.

And this is Amber—Martha Evarts Holden—a woman of sorrows and acquainted with grief; a woman who has warmed both hands at the fire of life; a woman whose joys are ecstasies and whose trials are stake and wheel. I wish I might tell of her home; of the two beautiful daughters and the manly son; of the good gray mother to whom this Queen of Bohemia is still a child. But after all, it may be enough to say of one, that he has influenced—and always for good—the largest number of those who love the genuine, who appreciate beauty, and who make sure of heaven by mixing it with earth.

LE ROY ARMSTRONG.

AMBER GLINTS.

CHAPTER I.

The other night I sat for an hour on a bench in a St. Paul park and looked out upon a scene of beauty, the memory of which lingers like the echo of a song in my heart. Beneath my feet lay stars and shadows. Above my head both shadows and stars were duplicated in softest infinitude. There was not a sound to break the stillness, save where an unseen fountain plashed its waters, or some idler, strolling home, whistled in the dewy dark. As far as eye could reach or ear could listen was silence, and nothing but silence, with scents of fading blossoms on the air. The great, passionate, bewildering town lay at my feet as quiet as some mighty soul in the arms of omniscient death. Not a tremor of its pain, not an echo of its joy reached me, and yet I knew that pleasure played its evanescent part, that white lips drank deep of sorrow's mystic wine, and sin flouted its scarlet shame behind the pall of shadow that overhung the city a hundred feet below the heights whereon I sat. Everything that was defiling, or harsh, or bitter to be borne was effaced by a touch as soft and all-obscuring as the snow. There was nothing but the tender allurement of an all-pervading peace in the picture upon which I gazed. The shading of a downy wing was never more delicate, the bloom on a wayside flower more darkly, deeply purple than the glamor of color revealed by the illumination of ten thousand sparkling lamps. And as I looked I thought to myself: "I wonder if when I have climbed the last height between my tired feet and the celestial city, leaving far behind me the bustling town where I have wept and struggled and endured, I shall look back upon a picture that gives so little evidence of it all. Will death's soft finger efface the harshness of the rugged outline and turn the shadows into bloom of plums? Shall all the anguish be forgotten in a peace that lingers like the touch of feathers in the dark, or the brush of mignonette sprays against a fevered face?

It is hardly worth while caring for present difficulties when to-morrow they shall be folded away and forgotten, as the defilements of yonder town beneath the outspread palm of holy night!"

* * * * *

Another day I took the trolley for Minnehaha Falls and lingered for an hour in a glen full of fern and the music of brooks. The fall itself reminds me of a mother standing with her finger on her lip at the doorway of her nursery. "Hush!" she seems to say. "Hush! for the little ones are asleep, and a rude footfall may disturb them. Make no noise, lest my darlings awaken and fill the valley with their fretful crying. Hush, I say, and evermore, hush, while the shadows lengthen and the new moon slips her light canoe through the blue silence of the sky." There is nothing one bit inspiring or grand in Minnehaha Falls, but I love to be there, and some day I am going again when nobody but the bee and I are on hand to listen to the whispered hush of falling water. You will seldom find such golden-rod as late summer has drifted into the valley. It is as though the Queen of Sheba had passed that way and tossed her yellow feathers and her sun-bright velvets on the rocks, weary of the sunset color on her bonnets and her gowns. I sat for a half hour on the banks of the Mississippi where Minnehaha pours her tribute into its rushing tide, and for the first time in my life felt the dignity of the great father of waters. The current was so swift as it rushed by the bank that the big logs on their way to the horrible saw-mills farther down the shore were carried at the rate of ten miles an hour. There was no light in the water, any more than there is in the skin of a Concord grape, and yet there was the same sense of power that is con-veyed by a beacon on a hill or sunshine at its meridian. The fascination of that terri-ble on-sweeping tide was so great that I think I should have bounded onto a log and sailed away from home and country had I not turned my back and climbed the hill.

* * * * *

Then I found the soldiers' home, a gay place, bright with flowers and with serene old men who seemed only waiting for me to kneel before them to confer a benediction. I have never seen richer marigolds than

were massed against the russet brown walls
of the fine old buildings, nor fairer colonies
of sweet fern and pansies than bordered the
garden walks. A seat on the brow of the
cliff commanded a view of the miles and
miles of river, woodland and reedy shore.
A crane soared into the evening sky and the
sound of a boatman's song made vesper
music. It was a grand place to sit and
muse, but musings must end as well as day-
light, and the ride back to the city in a noisy
trolley broke off the thread for the time being where it refused to join.

I don't like full moons. I love wan and
waning lights that half conceal and half
reveal the beauties of the midnight world.
Let others rave about the glory of over-
full harvest moons that drip with luscious
splendor, like some great juicy plum held
carelessly by a thoughtless hand, but give
to me the tender reserve of a moon from
which time has stolen something of its
youthful excess and meridian completeness,
leaving a chastened beauty in its stead, like

the smile on a face that has been washed by tears.

* * * * *

In the same way I don't like people when they are in the full pomp of popularity and power. They are wearisome in their perfection, like the undiminished splendor of a full moon in a cloudless sky. You long for something to be revealed; you would almost welcome a shadow to flit athwart the brightness that there might be the quality of a fresh surprise in what was yet to be.

* * * * *

I don't like the word policy. The moment you tell me that honesty is the best policy I am antagonized and almost prefer dishonesty. If you say to me that it is politic to be sweet-mannered I find myself shunning the appearance of hypocrisy which amiability of that sort too closely resembles. Tell me to be good for the sake of being good, and I will try right hard to behave myself, but tell me to be good because somebody is watching me and it will be to my advantage to make a good impression, and I shall, ten to one, disgrace my lineage. The fact is that we build up

character altogether too much after the
fashion of a farmer who should plant his
crops to please his neighbors, without con-
sulting his own predilections or prejudices.
"I will raise buckwheat, not because I like
buckwheat cakes, but because John Smith
does, and I might drive a better bargain
with John Smith some day should he
chance to drop in and eat a hot buttered
cake with me," is a no more senseless mode
of procedure than it is for me to be honest
and upright for no higher reason than because I shall have a better standing in the
community with that reputation tacked to
me.

Be good, be true, be pure, for your own
sake, and for the sake of that companion
you are going to spend eternity with—your
own self.

* * * * *

I am not an old woman, and yet I have
lived long enough to see the almost utter
decadence of some old-fashioned virtues.
Take politeness, for instance—simple, old-
fashioned politeness, that sprung from the
heart like a rose from the root. How little
we see of it nowadays. We see a great deal
of what you call company manners, learned

from a book of etiquette, perhaps, but the
kindly spirit that seeks to make things
pleasant for the humblest stranger, as well
as for the guest who comes in the van of a
trumpeting herald, is growing rarer each
year. What if it does cost a little trouble to
answer a question, or drop your task to direct a stranger; what is the use of being in
the world at all if not to lend a helping hand
where we can, and make folks happy. The
courtesy that is only shown to people we
know and to people who can respond perhaps in kind, is a spurious courtesy, as different from old-time politeness as a pink
made of muslin to a sweet carnation that
grows in the garden and woos the bees.

*   *   *   *   *

Let us give over clubs for awhile, and
start a training school for mothers. We do
not need anything so much in the world as
good mothers. As well expect the housekeeper to turn out a batch of good cookies,
if she makes them of sawdust and alum, as
to expect the children to develop into good
citizens without the right sort of mothers.
The right sort of mother knows where her
boy is all day long. She spends her time

entertaining him, rather than entertaining shallow-headed callers from everlasting to everlasting. She tells him stories, reads to him, and picks out tunes with him on the piano. She is "chummy" with him, too, and has his complete confidence. She doesn't allow her girls to go to the depot to see the trains come in, nor does she permit them to spend nights away from the guardianship of their own home. She is watchful at the same time that she is kind, loving always, but never languid in the performance of those duties which the vast responsibility of motherhood has laid upon her. Give us better mothers and the world will soon be full of better men and women.

There is something a great deal worse than hard work, and that is laziness. The man who toils until the big muscles of his arm stand out like hams, and his broad shoulders are bent like the branches of a pine under the force of a strong wind, is a king among his kind compared to the shiftless do-nothing, between whose feet are spun the cobwebs of sloth, and within whose lily fingers nothing more burdensome than a cigar ever finds its way. Give me a blacksmith any day rather than a dude. Work is hard, and sometimes thankless, but like tough metal, it is served to suit the needs of a strong man, and is better suited to that purpose than any entree or sweet confection.

* * * * *

Some day there is going to dawn a grand vacation morning for faithful toilers. Nobody ever worked honestly here but what he shall find, somewhere, an adequate compensation. And how blessed the thought that it is ours by right. No charity about it, dear toiler. It is your rightful due, bought with heavy eyelids and aching joints and desolate years of comfortless toil. We shall never have to thumb over our wretched little accounts there, and sigh, and sigh again, that we cannot force two and two to equal six. We shall never have to buy cheap things any more, because our horrid little incomes won't cover anything finer than 15-cent dress patterns. We shall never have to work like troopers all day, and not sleep forty winks all night, thinking over

how we shall buy shoes for all the kids on
Saturday night, besides scoring accounts
with the "butcher, the baker and the candle-
stick maker." When that vacation morning
dawns we shall find ourselves numbered
with those who carry banners and smite on
golden harps because they have "fought
the good fight" and endured to the end
without flunking.

* * * * *

I wonder what is the matter with the men
nowadays, and not only the men, but the
women and the girls! They are all getting
to be such tenderfeet! They can't endure
as much as a kitten did a few generations
ago. I have heard my grandmother tell
how the boys used to chop wood and hoe
corn; drive the oxen and thrash oats; walk
fifteen miles a day—not on wagers, but doing chores and hustling work—and yet the
average man of to-day kicks if the elevator
breaks down and he has to walk up three
flights of stairs! He is no account when
it comes to an emergency. He puts on his
overcoat in October, and wants the street
car heated if he rides a dozen blocks. And
the young women and the girls! It used to
be that a seventeen-year-old girl could run

a home, do a washing, and sit up until midnight entertaining her beau in the front parlor. I can remember the time when a poor man's daughter did the work and thought it the natural thing to do. But nowadays, if a man has to work hard for the maintenance of wife and daughters, they sit in the parlor and whine because servants are so incompetent in the kitchen. If by any manner of means they have to do the work it is a positively dreadful state of affairs, and they gain the commiseration of all their friends.

The trouble is that we overdo the luxuries of life. We have too much to eat; we have too many clothes; we live in too fine houses. If we would simplify about one-third of life as we live it we would develop new sinew and new strength, both of soul and body. Kick the stoves out of the street cars, tear the listing out of the windows, and take life a little more au natural, and there would be more men and women, and fewer editions du luxe in the human family.

* * * * *

The mild-mannered book agents (one of them was found in his lodging starved to

death the other day) come in for a large
share of my sympathy nowadays. If there
is anything worse than the vocation these
poor fellows follow so grimly and so pluck-
ily I don't want to know it. If you hand me
a bitter drug and tell me there is one still
more bitter it does not alleviate the un-
pleasantness of the dose in hand. A grade
lower than the book agent you find the itin-
erant in feather dusters, matches, and
whisk-brooms. Somehow these fellows always start a tear somewhere in my sensibilities. Mark the stolid endurance of a
joyless destiny that has drawn those set
lines about the man's mouth and deepened
his dago eyes with deeper shadows than
Italy's skies ever brooded over. Do you occasionally sell any of your wares, you non-
English, animal-browed son of Adam?
Does anyone ever say "Good morning" to
you or wish you god speed? Did anyone
ever wish you a merry Christmas, or remember your birthday, or look upon you
with tender and forbearing eyes? Was there
ever any respite from the horrible toting
around of feather dusters which nobody
wants? From door to door all day long—
God only knows where at night—finally

death, and a jolly round-up to a pauper's grave and then, what? Nobody knows, but you won't have to peddle feather dusters there—there is some comfort in that, isn't there, you product of the upper and nether millstones of ignorance and poverty?

Fifty years ago there were no telephones, no call for typewriters nor stenographers. The avenues of women's advancement were not opened, because in those days there were no lines of advance. As well say that the freight cars in the shop are maliciously held back and their utility belittled, when the roadbed is not yet laid through the wide country they are intended to traverse as to say that woman has been kept back and deprived of her rights until recent developments have launched her as the new type. The cars are ready when the track is laid. The woman was on hand when the opportunity presented.

* * * * *

Because a 'few women have battled for the day of their sex's recognition is no reason they should be especially glorified. As well laud the men for their eagerness to open the doors for the cars to run out of the shops. All their eagerness to do so was of no avail until the tracks were laid.

* * * * *

There never was a man or woman yet but what was bound to rise and progress and climb, provided the yeast principle was in their souls. As well try to keep leavened dough flat as to keep a great soul down. Poverty never yet forged a chain strong enough to hold a man prone, provided he was bound to rise.

* * * * *

Did you ever see a big Cunarder at its dock? She lies still because the fires are low and the engines at rest. But do you imagine there are iron links or steel grapples strong enough to hold her when the furnace fires are hot and the engines begin to throb? Anthony, nor Stanton, nor any other pioneer in the woman movement is to be thanked for woman's progress. When the opportunity came and the hour struck for sailing, she started for the wide sea.

* * * * *

Only now and then a public woman lends herself to methods so undignified as scolding and vituperation. The day for that has happily gone by, and yet, do you think a congress of men would be tolerated who should fling out so bitterly against the women as some of our women, in talking about men, yet do? Do not men always do our sex honor, sometimes with a lavish excess far beyond our merits? Have we not yet to complain of any lack of courtesy accorded to women as wives, mothers, sisters and sweethearts, where intelligent and honorable men are met together for the making of speeches? The lake would not be too wet a place to drive that convention of men into who should assail women as I have heard nice, motherly appearing women assail the men in "hen" conventions. He is a "brute," a "tyrant" and a "monster." He is "unclean," "despotic" and "impure." Now, all that is wrong, and sensible women know it.

* * * * *

There are bad men; there are bad women. There are peaches blown in the bud with worm-blight, but does that condemn all the orchards? I am tired of the attempt to blacken the character of the everyday, average man. He is a "brick" in business,

in social life and in love, and I like him. I
thank him for doing so much of life's uncomfortable work for me, and if he will be
so kind, I am perfectly willing that he should
go on building fires, killing chickens and
casting my vote at the polls while I am
kept safe and clean behind the scenes.

* * * * *

I wish that this old pen of mine could win
a magic power from somewhere to exploit
itself in behalf of sunshine-making rather
than trouble-breeding. The half of us spend
our lives incubating sorrow, as evil birds
brood goblin eggs. We fume and fret over
annoyances and cares that never would
chip their shells if we didn't hatch them. I
wish I could persuade the mother who
thinks every time the baby sneezes, or John-
nie gets his feet wet, or Mamie has the sore
throat that the funeral bell is already toll-
ing, to trust God more and not be such an
unbeliever in Providence. If you expect
evil, evil is bound to come just as these
summer evenings bats will enter if you put
a light in the window for them. What you
dread you will surely draw, and don't you
forget it. The man who goes out gunning

for hawks will see hawks. A thousand thrushes might sing to him under the clear blue sky, but he is after hawks, and he'll find them, too.

* * * * *

There is no doubt but what there is sorrow in the world and that somewhere on the road death crouches like a sleeping lion. But why shall we needlessly hunt for sorrow, and die a thousand times before our time for fear of the lion that won't waken until we reach him?

Who are the happy? I look about me sometimes and try to answer the question. First I take the married folks. Are they happy? Not one out of twenty. Why? Because they exact too much. Whisky itself has not wrought the marital woe that exaction has. Matrimony is a chain. You may pad it with velvet or wreathe it with flowers, yet it remains a chain. There is unwisdom in pulling it too tightly. As long as the slave does not feel his fetters he can

be comparatively happy, but let the steel
corrode his flesh and he becomes aware of
his thraldom.

When a woman goes through her husband's pockets on the sly she pulls at his
chain. When she sheds tears because he
walks downtown with a pretty neighbor she
pulls at his chain. When she sits up to
scold because he comes home late she pulls
at his chain. Such things may not be agree-
able for her to bear, but there are better
ways of holding a man than hauling him
along at the end of a chain. If I were a
married woman and had a husband who
neglected me, do you know what I would
do? I would begin all over again and lay
siege to his heart. I would make myself so
charming that before he knew it he would
fall in love with me for the second time.
There is no use denying it, men are queer.
They grow tired of what they possess and
are always reaching out after the fruit that
hangs high. There is something in a man's
nature that leads him to be always on the
lookout for fresh conquests. From the
time he begins to drive his dog in harness,
through the stage of liking to break colts,
all along the era of love-making, and away

down to old age, man wishes to be master of the situation and lord of a new possession. He loves his wife, no doubt, but after a few years she becomes an old story, and he begins to yearn for something newer and fresher. He doesn't mean to be exactly unfaithful, but he is like a man who leaves his Bible untouched to read the daily papers. The news is what he covets; the plan of redemption will do to save his soul and to base his hopes of heaven upon, but the columns of the 2-penny paper hold the current news, and that is what he demands for daily needs. If, then, when your husband is taken by the pretty looks of another woman you begin to "go her one better" on the question of beauty, you can keep him, provided he is worth the keeping—sometimes I doubt it. If she has pretty hair sit up all night to twist yours in paper, buy a new iron and spend many a golden hour getting up your own curls. If she has a lovely complexion, walk a mile a day and eat nothing but rye biscuits to freshen up your own roses. If she wears pretty gowns, get prettier ones of your own, even if you have to sandbag some one to get the money. Never give in and you'll win the day. But if you sit down and mope, with straight locks and red eyes, your husband will feel his chain to such an extent that he will run to the nearest blacksmith to get it filed off.

* * * * *

Sometimes I think there is a deeper lesson in such plays as "The Crust of Society" than we women perceive. Why do light women succeed in holding men as they do? It is because they take such pains to make the best of their beauty, because they are so daintily immaculate and charming. If good women were oftener fascinating they would gain a new empire in the world. Look about you at the nice little wives who do nothing but make apple-butter, heel stockings, seat pantaloons, and bake biscuit. They never rise out of their environment. They talk about nothing but domestic matters and hired help, with a sprinkling of physical ailments. The result is that they are less fascinating than so many setting hens. Now my advice to such women is, stretch your time so as to admit the opportunity to increase your fund of information a bit. Tuck the old stockings into the fire and get new ones if you can't get a chance otherwise to read the latest books, attend the bright plays, travel awhile, and keep young and fresh in soul and body. The man who is satisfied with a housekeeper for a wife ought to have married out of an employment bureau. Respectability is awfully tame as it is typified by half the women. An inhabitant from another star visiting this world and sampling its human products might judge of them, I think, something as a buyer might go through a wine merchant's stock.

"Here," says the salesman, "are our domestic wines; · they retail at 40 cents a bottle."

"Forty cents a bottle? Too cheap! No flavor! No sparkle! Give me the 'Green Seal.' I would rather pay high for what I drink, even if it goes to my head."

The flat stupidity of ultra-well-behaved people make them a drug on the market, even at 40 cents a bottle!

* * * * *

Not long ago I was spending the evening with one of the best women in the world. She is a church member, and a regular four-in-hand as to the Lord's work. We sat and talked by the light of a dim lamp, the chimney of which looked as though it had never been polished. A boy of about 12 years of age was trying to read by the poor light, but gave it up at last and went off to bed because he had nothing else to do. I wanted to say to that good woman, "My dear, lay aside your Bible to-morrow morning long enough to clean your lamp. One of the chief attractions of a saloon or any other iniquitous resort is the brilliancy of its illumination. Nobody ever turns in to take a drink at a dark and dingy place, do they? You want to set right about making home attractive for that growing boy of yours, and you will do well to begin at the lamps."

* * * * *

Another place where I went is presided over by an elder sister. She is the most dainty and immaculate of housekeepers and none enter or leave her home save with words of praise upon their lips. But there are never any playthings around; no nails, no hammer, nor precious tools dear to boyish hearts. No chair trains, nor steamboats made out of overturned tables. When her little brothers play they have to go out on the street—the house is too pretty to be turned over to children.

"Little woman," I want to say to this dear

girl, "turn right about face now, and start a new deal. Let the boys have all the good time they can in the old home, before they are driven too far away to find the road back again to the shelter. Put a billiard table in the basement and a gymnasium somewhere under the roof, and let the little fellows sail in. Time will come, perhaps, when you will see the mistake you have made in keeping the place too orderly and too immaculate. God grant it may not be too late."

*   *   *   *   *

I wonder if the time will ever come when we shall learn not to judge by appearance? When we shall be wise enough to look for the circumstance that colors the fact? A dozen times a day this thought occurs to me, until I feel tempted to hire the Auditorium and preach to every man, woman and child who can be entreated to hear me the supreme folly of hasty judgment. Take a case in instance, and as I record it I offer up a prayer that it may be read by the right party. Not long since I received a charming letter from a stranger inviting me to lunch somewhere away on the Rock Island suburban line. According to the practice of

years I mislaid the letter, or stuck it away
in a pigeon-hole from which only the processes of time shall ever dislodge it. Of
course, judging from my silence, the lady
who sent me the pleasant invitation thinks
me discourteous, rude—everything that I
try not to be. Otherwise she would write
again, giving me the benefit of a doubt.
Probably I shall never be able to vindicate
myself, and whenever the name "Amber"
floats through that little home it will leave
a trail of smoke! This is only one of many
instances of daily occurrence wherein a
charitable judgment would bring about a
satisfactory explanation. More lovers have
been parted and more estrangements
brought about by lost letters and addresses
than by any other method known to the evil
one. Never believe ill of anyone until you
face the fact bodily, with no go-betweens of
letters, silence or contradictory evidence to
bias your judgment.

Bargain! How I hate the word! And
this is an age of bargains. We cheapen
everything and call it a benefit to mankind.

It is not conducive to the proper spirit of ambition to cheapen wares of any kind, either spiritual or temporal. The moment you begin to bargain for a ware that moment a something sordid enters your soul which the king's soap can never eradicate. Enhance your values rather than cheapen them. Render it worth something to attain a prize, and urge a man to effort rather than to ease. If there isn't enough vim in a man to pay an equivalent for what is fine, let him go without. Roses, sonnets, moons and dewfalls are nature's gifts to man, but if nature should begin to dicker about her roses and her dew the charm of each would be sullied. Either be bountiful as nature is and give good things freely, or be just and make men strive that they may appreciate. The moment you say to a man I will give you for a cent what has cost me 10 cents to furnish, you not only cheapen your goods but you cheapen art, and, what is worse still, you cheapen yourself. I would rather be found robbing birds' nests than hunting bargains.

When I think of all the good times there are in this world which you and I might be in if we only had the good sense to avail ourselves of our opportunities, I am inclined to think that we are not to be commiserated so much after all if we fail to have our good time oftener.

* * * * *

Take this glorious week of weather, for instance, out in the country. If the opportunity were offered you, suddenly, to leave your city home and settle yourself for a fortnight in close vicinity to the woods and the beautiful lake country, would you avail yourself of the chance? Oh, no; you would raise a thousand objections, and before you were done with them the opportunity would be gone like one of the foam wreaths out yonder on the waves. You would have no nice clothes (I am talking to the women), or you would not be able to put aside your household duties, or the children would be needing you at night to help with their lessons, or your husband's people would be coming to town to do their shopping. Some trivial thing or other would be sure to interfere with your outing until your chance for deliverance from the grind of daily care would be gone like the wind from the poplars.

If one sat on shore and waited for some trig little boat from off the sea to sail up to the strand, draw one into it by some method of affinity unknown to science and carry one off to Spain, don't you think one would grow gray-headed and wan before the voyage commenced? It is just as silly, and just as hopeless, to wait for some full-rigged opportunity to draw near and force you on board. Without some effort on your part you will never set sail. You will never go anywhere if you do not arise and go. Leave things undone, if need be. Bother the duties! Shoot the obligations! Let their father help the children! Just you get up and go!

It matters little how I got there! Do you suppose anybody will stop us, when after long journeying we reach heaven's country, with an inquiry as to the route we took? No, my dear; we may take the Baptist water voyage, the Methodist limited, or the elevated road of the high church—it will make precious little matter when once we stand on the margin of the silver tide or stoop to gather our first asphodel.

I have been here three days—that is, I
had been when the summons came that
called me home. Oh, but three hundred
years would not be too long to remain in so
beautiful a country. The poplar trees have
turned to jonquils and all the maples into
ragged carnations, spilling fire for dew.
Every instant I expect to see the sky
shrivel in the fervent glow of a heatless con-
flagration, and, looking through, see Mary
swinging her lily bough about the heads of
dreaming seraphs. Wild talk, perhaps you
think, but just slip your cable and run away
into the woods and meadowlands one of
these glorious October mornings and see if
I paint the picture too highly.

* * * * *

Oh, worry, worry! You are responsible
for more gray hairs and wrinkles than age.
You have penciled more brows with tell-tale
lines than years have ever thought of doing.
Shall I tell you what I think about the disposition to worry? It reminds me of what
it would be if a company of convivial souls
should sit down to a banquet and fall to
weeping and wailing because this time next
year they may go to bed hungry. For

heaven's sake be thankful for to-day's dinner and enjoy it. Let to-morrow's dinner
rest in the hands of the gods; they'll be sure
to wheel things into line if you trust 'em.
Do your duty. Grasp your end of the line
and pull. Accomplish all you can, and never
fret. When providence sees such a fellow
on the road providence is sure to harness up
and meet him on the way with a two-seated
surrey and a lap robe. Sure as fire is fire
and frost is frost, heaven helps the brave
and piles stumbling blocks in the way of
the cowardly hearted who complain over
nothing.

It was long past the dinner hour and the
restaurant was deserted. I staggered in
with my bundles and asked for tea and trim-
mings. The waiter who responded was very
straight, very black, and very attentive. I
had but to look "spoon," "napkin," "salt,"
and he produced the same. He relieved me
of my cloak and kept an eye on my slippery
bundles as they skated from my lap across
the shining floor. I began to feel that I

must tip that waiter, or go out into the night branded as a skinflint.

So I opened my purse and took out a coin. It was Canadian, and I had experienced many trials with it. I had carried it about with me for months and nobody would accept it in change.

"This waiter," thought I, "is a man, and consequently has more nerve than a meek, down-trodden woman such as I. To him I will give the Canadian coin as a tip and let him try his luck." So I slipped it underneath my plate and rose to depart. As I neared the cashier's desk I found the cashier had stepped out for an instant, so I stood impatiently awaiting change. Down stepped my "nervy" waiter. "I can accommodate you," said he, and changed my dollar, handing me back my Canadian coin. I was so stunned by its reappearance, and also by the strategic workings of that waiter's giant intellect, that I made no murmur, but turned upon my heel and strode forth into the night. That waiter will make his mark yet. Such smartness merits recognition. I feel like a feeble, commonplace clod when I meet such meteoric intellects as his, and humbly creep to my own place among

the dullards and laggards of earth born
without mercantile instincts.

Once, in the long ago years, when every
bird that sang was a thrush, and every day
that dawned was overshone by sparkling
suns, I was one of a party of voyagers down
the Pacific Ocean to Santa Cruz.

After a night of storm there came a soft,
gray dawn filled with perfume. From some
out of sight and inexplicable quarter an
odor as of a rose garden wet with dew over-
brimmed the air.　There was no land in
sight, or at least there was but a faint haze
of blue cliffs, which might be clouds or
might be hills, and yet our senses were en-
wrapped in balm, and every breath we drew
was a dreamy delight.

·For an hour or more we sailed across the
slow-illuming sea before the ship's prow
was brought to land and we were allowed
to take a run over the fields during the process of fruit embarkation. A little way
back from the lifted barrier of the sea cliff
we found the source of that delicious, flow-
er-scented morning air, a plantation of

roses, far as the eye could reach. Nothing in all the enchanted world about us but roses. The thorn-set Cherokee, bedecked with creamy petals like crushed and crumpled gold, the superb damask with its inner heart of flame, the stately white rose, a drift of snow caught and upheld by a wand of green, the blush rose with its memories of long ago, the button rose in its trim little jacket of verdure, the Baltimore belle with haughty head held high, the brilliant prairie queen with its soulless splendor. Every kind of rose one ever heard of, or handled, or loved, was there in such countless numbers that although one tarried to pick the live-long day the colony of blooms would never be perceptibly decreased. And from this garden there stole forth on every breeze the aroma that had made the dawn so beautiful and greeted us far out at sea, before the sight of land had gladdened our eyes.

In recalling the incident my heart quickens with a fond regret for the sight once more of those wind-swept acres, haunted through silver dawn, and golden noon, and dewy dusk, with humming birds and honey bees. Unvisited by me forevermore, the frail things blow and wither and droop upon their stately stems throughout the circuit of the constant years. Unplucked by me, the sweet buds look from behind their lattices of green, like ladies at their window-blinds, and waft their odorous breath like smiles upon the air.

I shall never see that land of flowers again, perhaps, but no barren lot in life, no deprivation and no future pain shall ever rob me of the memory of that long ago morning spent among the roses.

It is many years no doubt since some loving hand planted the first bush in that plat of ground. Perhaps it was a young wife, herself transplanted to a pioneer home, who amid a gentle rain of home-sick tears set out the little rose slips brought from the dear New England home garden, and with an aching heart and a zealous care watched them multiply and spread from year to year. Each season a host of new shoots appeared, developed quickly under those balmy skies, until the profusion overran all limits and changed the wilderness into a garden of delight. The enclosure came to be looked upon as a place set apart, a spot wherein to grow roses for the mere joy their beauty and their perfume might yield. The plowman who

should seek to devastate that plat of verdure,
or the farmer who might be tempted by love
of lucre to turn it into profit by uprooting
the rose tendrils and filling their places with
grain or garden produce, would be regarded
as a desecrater of consecrated ground. The
roses long since pre-empted a claim on that
acre of land, and woe to the vandal hand
that should seek to evict them. No other
flower grew within that garden place; no
vines, however fruitful, were allowed to
cumber the ground where all day long and
through the hush of starry Southern nights
drifted the loosened petals of ten thousand
roses waving their languid heads in sweet
content. The space wherein they grew was
a spot of earth set apart from sordid uses
for the reign of beauty, purity and perfume.

And so I think in this life of ours are the
sheltered gardens where girlhood buds and
blossoms, and casts, in time, the benignant
influence of unsullied womanhood. What-
soever things are lovely and without guile
should environ that spot where young womanhood holds her gracious reign. Whatso-
ever influences are pure and precious should
emanate from thence, so that away out on
the stormy and restless reaches of life, we

who wander and are sore beset by sin and sorrow shall be comforted and made to rejoice unwitting, as our spirits catch the perfume from those fair gardens that lie along the Eastward shore of time's restless sea.

See to it then, O, young girls, whoever and wherever you be, that read this little sketch of mine to-night, that you set to work planting rose slips in the neglected gardens of your souls. Abjure unlovely things. Stop being a little bit bold and common. Begin to flaunt less and bloom more. Do lovely things whenever you have the chance, and the chances lie thicker along the way, let me tell you, than you imagine. Trifling courtesies, off-hand services, gentle words and pleasant glances will start the roses growing. If you have been in the habit of powdering your faces and chewing gum and laughing at smutty jokes, and flirting on the streets, and lingering around depots and in public places; if you have allowed yourself to grow a trifle fast in a fast city and in a fast age, turn right about face now and begin to be womanly and modest and reserved and sweet. Faithful endeavor will soon bring the perfume into your life, and evolve within you a rare

and lovely womanhood, even as from the
most delicate cuttings are produced in time
the most perfect coronals of bloom.

Did you ever think that it is not he who
reaps the harvest who is responsible for it?
It is the sower of the seed, the instigator of
the small beginning, who is accountable.
The cross word you or I may say this morning may not produce its harvest of ill-tem-
per at once, but after we have left the house
and gone about our daily business, the
wrangle of the home life is but the resultant
harvest of the seed we dropped from an
idle tongue. I wish some thought of this
kind could keep us serene and sweet! I
wish there was anything short of a change
of heart and saving grace that could keep
back the bitter word or the sarcastic speech
when both are so surely the seeds of a
wretched harvest. If somebody will tell
me how to live one day without dropping
a single word to be regretted at bed time, I
will send that person a white hyacinth in a
silver pot!

CHAPTER II.

There was once a Brave Soul set out on its journey through the world. Panoplied with the glory of that radiant land that lies the thither side the sunrise sky, the Brave Soul started on its wanderings as a paradise bird darts from a thicket of tropical bloom, or as a fountain seeks the upper air from its bed of velvet mosses. There was no shadow on its beauty, no undertone of sadness in its song. Around about it the beautiful low lands of childhood lay, rimmed softly with azure hills above it, the unclouded sunshine rippled like a golden flood, and in all the land there was no sound of sorrow, nor frost of remorseful complaint. The Brave Soul flew with a strong wing, nor stopped its pinion until, the vales of childhood passed, it hovered a space above the hills that girdle the land of youth. Upon every tree that cast its verdure across the songful slopes grew fruits that mocked in

luscious beauty the apples of Hesperides
and the grapes of sunny Spain. But stoop-
ing to gather and eat of the fruit it turned
to substanceless moisture on the lips, or
faded at the first touch of the eager hand.
And the Brave Soul, nothing troubled, flew
on until it passed out of the sunshine into
a region of wandering lights and winds.
There was restlessness in the air like the
passage of an unheralded storm, and in the
tops of the mighty trees a host of dark-
winged birds sat ever complaining to the
waning sun and to a wan and wasted moon.
But the Brave Soul took no account of
throbbing storm nor of chattering bird of
evil omen, but flew on its way upheld by
the wings of an undaunted courage. And
as the way stretched farther and farther
from the dells and dales of childhood's land
of delight the clouds thickened between the
Brave Soul's steadfast eye and the blue
above, and now and again the cry of a hungry beast of prey smote the ear from im-
penetrable thickets that belted the lengthen-
ing way. In the path of the Brave Soul a
spirit of evil, called the Demon of Unfaith,
often contested for right of way and darkened the air with its somber visage. But

4

the Brave Soul trembled not, nor yet was dismayed, but singing ever of the land from whence it came, kept flying straight towards Heaven. It saw the pitiless storm of life beat down the faint blessing of hope, so that the golden fruitage lay like withered stubbles beneath the darkened harvest moon. It saw untimely frosts descend upon the vineyards where the purple vintage of joy and faith and peace smiled back to the constant sun, and lo! the grapes were blighted on the branch, and the wine of consolation ran no more from within the presses. It saw the desert spaces over which a vertical sunglare beat remorselessly, and within whose limits not even a grass blade waved to the passage of the sterile wind. But with all, the Brave Soul kept its bright spirit undaunted, and evermore flew singing straight to the bosom of infinite love. But finally there came a day when even the Brave Soul drooped on broken wing, and over its fainting head the shadow of voiceless and comfortless despair fell heavily. For when it came to the acre of the dead, sown thick with graves and wept upon forevermore by human tears, in that abode of desolation it saw its mate flutter

like a loosened leaf from a wind-startled
branch. And although it tarried in its flight
and called with an exceeding mournful cry,
for alas! the cry came from the depths of a
breaking heart, the silent mate lifted never
again its quiet wing, nor looked with yearning love from out the shut lids of its tender
eyes.   So here in the domain of death,
through which all souls, both ignoble and
brave, must pass on their flight towards
heaven, even the Brave Soul tarried and
could not arise and press onward for many
and many a day. The distant land of Paradise seemed less than nothing to the Brave
Soul while its gentle mate lay pulseless beneath the shadow of death's dark wing, and
although the bright ones gathered in the
western sky in flocks like clouds of ruby and
violet and gold, the Brave Soul neither
looked nor listened beyond the confines of
the land of graves, but fluttered like a
wounded lark entangled in the meshes of
the summer grass. Perhaps there came a
time when the Brave Soul resumed its flight
towards heaven, but when last I passed
that way its wing was wet with earth dews,
and the gaze of its once clear and fearless

eye could lift itself no higher than the turf-covered verge of a newly-made grave.

Where has spring gone? The other day she was here in the glow of a robin's breast and the gush of its liquid song. She loitered about the gardens and left a foot-print in the crocus beds. She drifted down the wind, a soft cloud for her boat, a strip of blue cloud for her pennon. She met us in the morning and laughed in our face with radiant sunshine. She parted from us at evening leaning over the parapet of gold in the western sky, and throwing us a balmy kiss from clouds like rosy finger-tips; but she has vanished utterly from our midst, and a vixenish spell of weather is abroad that pinches our fingers and scolds like a shrew. But drink of the wine of frosty mornings I pray you while you may, for when dog-days come and we wilt and wither, and simmer and droop, won't we long for the zest of a frosty flagon again? By the way, what a thankless, grumbling set of mortals we are. Never a spring comes around but a wail ascends to the very stars that the late frosts have surely nipped the fruit. If a season's rainfall exceeds the average, then the wet has rotted the potatoes; if there is no rain, but a chain of bright and cloudless summer days slips along the strand of weather, then the drouth has killed the crops. When the autumn rolls round the early frosts are sure (in our croaking estimation) to blight the yield of fruit, or deferred cold is the attributed reason for malaria and unhealth. To find a man perfectly content with what nature gives him in the shape of weather would be to find a greater marvel than any dime museum boasts.

I have sometimes thought that if the Lord means to destroy a man he first makes him moderately rich — gives him just enough money to turn his head, and then leaves him to his own devices. What such a man is not capable of in the way of meanness is not worth mentioning. A millionaire snob is bad enough, although he is of full growth and can be tolerated, but the consequentiality that stalks up and down the earth like a bantam in the midst of eagles and fills the air with feathers and squeaks is a sight to make men weary. Do you not, all of you, know just such people? Some of them live in the suburbs of large cities because rents are cheap, not because they have any love for pure air and nature. They form themselves into cliques and call themselves the best society, when they know no more about the "best" than a city alderman knows about the court of the king. They apply the standard of the purse, never that of the brain. They will frown upon a young man who publicly associates with anyone out of their "set," but overlook the fault if he ruins a poor girl quietly and without exposure. Breach of purity is more readily condoned by them than breach of etiquette. They tolerate dudes so everlastingly fragile of brain and limb that they ought to be kept in cotton like Florida orange-buds, yet look with disfavor upon young men and women who work for a living. They patronize the arts in the same way that a butterfly patronizes a rose. They sing a little and dance a great deal, and talk together with about the same display of wisdom and wit that characterize the council of a herd of sheep or of a flock of crows. They look down upon people who are not willing to go through life like peas in a pod or like tallow-dips in a mold. Their enthusiasms are well enough so far as they go, but they never unfurl more than a square inch of bunting at a time. Their value in this wide world of action is very much what the value of tin soldiers would be on a field of battle —very neat, very shining and correct, but nothing but toys after all.

They have enough money to keep horses and carriages, but whom do they take to ride? The poor and the sick, the discouraged and the forlorn? Not to any monotonous extent. Their favors are not given without due regard to future returns. They do generous things in the same way that they give wedding presents—with an eye to value received.

If there is a large family of daughters dependent upon one of these moderately affluent papas, they toil not, and never, by any manner of means, spin out the solution of the problem of their own support. They pinch and turn and fight like cats behind the scenes to secure new frocks and jewels, but carry themselves in public like princesses of a long line of ancestral kings. They beat down the wages of those who serve them, and run up big bills at the stores for tormented papa to pay, but as for lending a hand to pull their over-burdened bark up stream, they would sooner die. They never carry bundles, and the sight of another woman doing so kindles their infinitesimal spark of humor into the flame of feeble hilarity. They might meet a fellow-creature on a plank in the middle of the sea, or in an oasis of Sahara, and never presume to speak without formal introduction. Oh, I am tired of talking about them! If I was the wind I'd blow them away like dandelion disks. Empty-headed, with hearts of steel and bowels of brass! May the Lord who allows such shoddy folks to live appoint them a corner to themselves in the "sweet by-and-by."

Did you ever stop to think what would become of us all if some day the world should crash off the track like a freight running on lightning express time? It would be something like the air in the immediate vicinity of a threshing machine, I'm thinking, with stars for chaff and solar system for dust. But then the beauty of it would be that we would all go together. The lone-

liness of individual dying is the worst feature of death to me. The idea of taking the
trip all alone seems so dreary. But to go
out of the lighted depot into the darkness
of the night by the car-load is not so bad.
Ah, well! they go fast, these years of life,
don't they? And they will go faster and
faster yet, like horses nearing home, until
the footman shall descend from his box and
politely hold the door for the restless inside
passenger to alight at the journey's end.
All right, old fellow, the journey has been
an up-hill one at best, and the dust has gotten well into our eyes—pray God it has not
gotten into our hearts—and many of us are
glad to rest awhile, and after—?

Have you ever, amidst the stir and bustle
of busy morning, when cocks were crowing
and cattle lowing, when the sound of labor
awoke upon the air from its many sources,
and there was no silence anywhere in Nature's busy realm, caught the surpassing
sweetness of a sudden bird song, shrill and
sweet, yet full of strange and mystic sadness? Such a song makes itself vocal in my
heart to-night and I know full well its echo

will find a lodgment in many another breast than my own. A song for the vanished one! A song for the spirit that like a lark, uprose from out these low earth-grasses and winged its flight through heaven's portals! A song for the child we loved whom God loved too, and whom He has recalled to be with Him in Paradise! A song for the eyes that shone, now drooped forever beneath their soft dark lids! A song for the golden hair, for the sweet white brow, for the frank young mouth, where "smiles lit outward their own sighs!" A song for the nestling cheek so soft and warm, for the rose-leaf touch of the little hands, for the restless feet so strangely, terribly still! A song for the sweet dead breast whereon dead lilies lie! A song for courage and strength and trust to outlive our loneliness and uplift our heads again from the bitter storm! A song for sweet assurance surely given, that

> "Love, that else might fade,
>   By Death immortal made—
> Spurns at the grave, leaps to the welcoming
>   skies,
>   And burns a steadfast star to steadfast
>   eyes."

There was the usual manifestation of alarm as the fire patrol came darting down the street to the tune of clanging bells. People drew out of the way, and a few timorous women screamed and sought shelter in stairways. With a mad pace like a colt let loose in the clover the big red wagons swung down the avenue and halted before a building that was smoldering with barricaded fire. From every window gray chiffon, deepening into black, floated, and there was a sultriness in the air like the portent of a tempest.

"Let us stop and watch this fire," said the poet, "it is bound to be a good one. So much smoke as that fathers a big blaze."

So we stopped close to one of the hose carts and waited.

Ladders were run up the wall, like wooden webs, to be quickly mounted by brave men who played with danger as kittens play with yarn. More wagons dashed up the street, and the air grew full of clamor as a buckwheat field of bees. Hose after hose was turned upon the building that still belched smoke from its many windows, and stood up gaunt and gray against the illumination of the night. Suddenly a tongue of flame lapped over the roof's edge, and was as quickly withdrawn. Then from the topmost peak a flag of fire floated as though swung by a hellish hand, and swift to obey the summons, the night filled with a crimson host. It halted a moment, seeking a foothold, then with a shriek noiseless to our ears but vocal no doubt in those regions where fire is king, the flaming legion scattered like a colony of leaves in a gale, and instantly the night was full of disintegrated fire, as a turnpike fills with wayside dust. There was a blizzard at that moment in hell, and fire fell for snow; there was a shower just then along the banks of the Stygian River, with sparks for rain. The color of tulips, tawny cupped and filled to the brim with ruby light; the delicious mingling of flaming yellow and sea-depth green met in these flames that caught the night in their embrace and flung aside its robe of darkness. Hurrah! and huzzah! seemed voiced upon those tongues that licked up the lesser lights of the town as a tiger laps blood, until it seemed as though a tornado of sound, like passion in a mute's breast, shook at the very center of the voiceless clamor. "This is splendid!" cried the poet, and stepping

aside bought out the stock of a flower
vendor that we might pin roses upon our
gowns in remembrance of a half hour's tarrying in the court of the king.

Sometimes I have moods when I think
the most blessed lot that could overtake a
self-respecting woman would be to be shut
up in a dungeon and guarded by a polite
keeper. There is something so revolting
to me in this mad rush of the fin de siecle
woman for recognition! Great heavens,
my dear, haven't we had all the recognition necessary? Must we be carried along,
like the fly on the wheel of the chariot, until
there is only a memory left in the heart of
man of such women as that grand saint in
New England, whom, by the way, I don't
know that I ever told you of. She didn't
make much of a record outside of her home
while she lived, but I think no sweeter sermon was ever preached than her grave has
preached for twenty years in a little hillside
graveyard in New Hampshire.

"She was so pleasant." That is what is
lettered on the headstone, and I would rath-

er merit that encomium than almost any other the world could grant me. Think of that, ye wheel riders and voters, ye riotous formulaters of discord in clubs, ye office seekers and suffrage howlers. What is going to be the epitaph that the hand of truth letters upon the graves of more than one-half of your number? Perhaps it shall be said of you: "She was so smart," "So aggressive," "So hard to get the best of," "So expert at bicycling," and "So handy with bloomers." But very few of you shall ever smile up from underneath the daisy roots to feel some one part the grass on your graves and read, with half a laugh and half a sob, "She was so pleasant!" Bless her dear heart! For not many of the advanced copies of the new woman are very pleasant, to my reckoning. They are hedged about with a false dignity, they bristle with a spurious independence, they are lurid with aggressiveness and too awfully smart at repartee for comfort. I don't want to be a fool, and I don't like fools; but if women of the sweet Alice type are counted as fools, I will fall in line rather than keep up with this latter-day procession of greedy seekers after position, fortune and fame. Wouldn't you rather be possessed of a disposition that should make a friend weep to remember your name twenty years after your body had gone back to dust, than be recalled to recollection by a photograph taken en route up the boulevard on a bicycle on your way to an Australian booth to cast your vote for Mayor of Chicago?

How tired we are! How ready to fold the arms and let the old boat drift! How indifferent to the fate of the weather-beaten thing! Let it go; we have pulled at the heavy oars long enough. Our hands are callous, our head droops. There is no sunshine above where the torn clouds fly, no brightness below where the dark currents whirl. What is the use of forever tugging away to keep a miserable old scow headed up stream, when unseen and cruel forces are always dragging it down the dark waters of defeat? We started out with high courage, but the currents have been too strong for us. The bit of bunting we

carried at the mast-head went overboard
long ago.   The name of the boat, in gilded
letters, "Hope," is washed illegible by briny
seas.   Lo, the thunder of the breakers just
ahead of us in the fog! Is it not easier to
drift on the ledge than to keep pulling?
Only a plunge, that is all, and then—who
shall number the years of our content?
Who shall tell over the sweet endurance of
our rest?   This is the way the bravest of
us talk when the January thaws come, and
all the crystal winter world is turned to sod-
den clouds and drizzle.   This is the way we
talk when the girl has put too much sale-
ratus in the muffins, or undercooked the
veal. But let the west wind get after the
clouds as a Scotch collie dog gets after a
sheep, and send them flying through the
celestial meadow-lands and over the horizon bars; let the old cook go, and get a new
one who will be more careful about the
muffins, and how quickly the aspect of life
changes!

I met a little woman to-day, all draggled
and rumpled and wet. We stood upon the
street corner in the rain, two sketches from
life, as it were, of the most wretched women
in Chicago.   The hair-pins had all fallen out

of my back hair, and my head was Medusa-
like. I had no umbrella. I wore a short
dress and the martyr's arctics. The appearance of the little woman was even more
doleful. She carried an umbrella, but it
leaked, and had smeared her face with olive
tints. She was thin, and chilly, and limp.

"Well," said I, "this is awful weather,
isn't it?"

"Indeed it is," said she, "but it doesn't
make much difference to poor folks what
sort of weather it is."

"No, indeed, it does not," said I. "Sunny
weather doesn't bring in money to pay the
bills any faster than stormy weather does."

"How are you?" asked she.

"Sick," answered I; "I'm going to see the
doctor now."

"I have had neuralgia so badly of late,"
said she, "that I am all worn out."

"I hear that there is an epidemic of diph-
theria," said I.

"I thought the baby had it last night,"
said she, "but it was croup."

"Small-pox and cholera are expected to
visit Chicago this coming season," said I.

"Yes," said she. "Could you lend me a
quarter?"

I dived into the depths of my bag and produced some cracker crumbs and two cents.

Then we both wiped our eyes—she with a veil that accentuated the olive tints; I on the windward side of my mitten.

"Good-bye," said I.

"Good-bye," said she, and the sound of my departing arctics as I plunged on my way was hushed in the breath of her heavy sighs.

A few hours later the wind had changed and it had stopped raining. Enough blue appeared in the sky to make trousers for forty tailors. The little woman and I met again.

"Lovely afternoon," said she.

"Glorious," said I.

"Where are you going?" asked she.

"Around to the florist's to look at the flowers," said I.

"I have just been to get my new sappho bang," said she; "how does it look?"

"Lovely," said I; "do you like my new veil?"

"You are just adorable in that color," said she; "let's go around to Chopley's and get a fry."

"All right," said I; "but we'll buy a pot of primroses first; I believe spring is really coming."

Now nothing on earth shifted our tune out of the minor into crisp and sparkling major but the change in the weather. To be sure, the leaving off of the arctics may have had something to do with the uplifting of my spirits, for I verily believe there is something uncanny about a woman who can be gay in arctic overshoes. It is like attempting to say bright things to a deaf man, or taking a moonlight ride in a west side street car, to strive to keep the head light with those architectural monstrosities on our feet.

Ah, but my dear, I do not intend to treat the actual sorrows of life lightly. I know how many hearts to-day are aching, which no shifting wind nor blooming spring can ever make merry again. I, for one, am dumb before the mighty preponderance of mere physical suffering in the world. From Chatterton, dying in his garret, to the poor lost dog in the street, or the tortured horse in his nosebag, it is anguish, despair and torment all the way.

When you and I get rich, my dear, as some day we surely shall, when the long-delayed fleet of expectation sails into port, we will know just whom to help of the hosts of needy ones who surround us. We will slyly pay the vexing bills for some of those dear people who have grown gray in the struggle to make a four-foot income cover six-foot requirements. We will take tired invalids who have lain all their lives in pain away to the country where they can hear the bobolinks in the clover and see the great and infinite sky. We will snatch old gentlemen out of stuffy shops where they toil and give them a pipe and an easy chair on a southward lying piazza. We will gather up whole armfuls of tired mothers who have fought valiantly the battle to keep their fatherless children nourished and happy, and we will build a home for them somewhere where plumbers and coal dealers and grocery men never intrude with bills. They shall forget how to spell care, and their happy dialect shall know no such words as "dues," or "can't afford it," or "monthly payments."

We are not rich, the more's the pity, but

there are lots of folks who are and here is love's opportunity for all such.

I am tired of the ceaseless waltz of events. I want to go back and be a protoplasm. I want to be a barnacle on a South Sea Island rock, and let the full Pacific tides wash over me, and the southern suns steep me in infinite calms of laziness. I want to forget that Mr. Yerkes ever dreamed about a cable-car and materialized his dream, or that there is such a thing as a telegraph, or a fire-alarm, or a steam-engine in the world. My brain aches with the effort to keep up with the pace of events. I have felt this way aboard swift-rushing cars. Should experience the same sensation, I think, tied to the tail of a comet sparkling through space. Give me the rest that lurks in clover blossoms and shadow-haunted woods, and you may take my place in Vanity Fair; you may fall into file with the votaries of fashion and pleasure, beating with tireless feet the round of overflowing days. I wish I were a bird, to spread my wings and fly away to the top of a tall elm tree or a mountain pine, leaving forever this crazy world, and steering my feathered sails straight into the upper blue, dipping my plumy oars in far-off songful seas of air. I'd go to Oregon, where neither the devil nor a wood-chopper had been before me, and I'd find some forest so vast and deep that even the flutter of a falling leaf could be heard for miles in the still air, and there I'd build me a nest of silence, drink sunshine for wine, and never grow old. And when death came I'd turn into an angel without any more fuss than it takes for a bud to burst into a blossom. I'd have no funeral, nor crape, nor mourning friends, no floral display nor out-door parade of hearse and followers, but I'd simply die and be done with it, as "morning changes into noon." That fancy suggests another. Do you know I think it would be rather difficult to change a wide-awake, public-spirited citizen of earth into a domestic angel. He would always be coming back and poising his wing like a butterfly's in the air, to see how the world was faring. He wouldn't take half as much interest in the new home as in the old. How would it seem, I wonder, to visit earth with the gyves of mortality stricken from our faculties and the dust of limitation brushed from our vision; to watch the green globe like a bubble in the sunshine, floating on its way amid the stars? Imagine an angel poised above us this moment, what would he see, and how would it all seem to him? Would he laugh, or brush away a tear with his unlaundried plumage, and soar back to the heavenly country, glad that his race on earth was run forever? Dimpled with dells, and carved into hills, starred with waters and fringed with forests, I think this brisk little planet would seem a very nice pocket edition of paradise itself, for never tell me that heaven can be any fairer than earth shall be one day, if dusted of sorrow and sin.

I have been gradually learning to leave a great many things that used to take up a good deal of my attention to God. The consciousness that He is abundantly able to attend to His own concern has taken considerable of a load off my mind. For instance, I used to fret a good bit because of evil-doers, but since I have come to a full appreciation of the fact that God will at-

tend to the sinner's case better than I can I
manage to get lots more comfort out of life.
It is no more concern of mine what other
people do than the condition of your preserve cellar is to your neighbor. These may
be bad all the way through and those may
be just beginning to spoil, but all that is
their Maker's concern and nobody else's.
My neighbor's wife may wear an ill fitting
gown, but if I look well after the fit of my
own raiment that is all I am responsible for.
She has to wear the dress, not I, and any
interference of mine is an impertinence.
The matter lies between her and her dress-
maker. In the same way the fellow that
lives next door to you may be the meanest
sort of a reprobate, but his morality is a
matter between himself and God. Any interference of yours is ill timed and superfluous. When we learn to treat humanity
as individual and not composite we shall
do much to solve the problem of universal
peace. Whatever I do is my affair. The
same to you, my dear, and heaven help us
to be wise in our choice and honest in living
up to it. If I sin it is my own concern; my
life is mine and I must live it, yielding at
last the keys of my stewardship from my

own hand, and not from yours. I am answerable directly to God for my blunders, my shortcomings and my sins, and I'm glad of it. I'd rather take my chances with Him than with any fellow-creature judgments.

*   *   *   *   *

What a mistake we make when we express any dread of judgment day! In reality the only salvation for poor, groping, sin-shattered humanity lies in the fact that God is to be our judge, and that He is just. There is more comfort to be gotten out of that one word "just" than we often stop to consider. What human censor was ever absolutely unbiased? What earthly tribunal is without corruption? It is an exceeding pleasant thought to me, then, that I am going to be finally judged by one who knows me best of all. I am going to be cross-examined by no whipper-snapper attorney of flesh and blood, but my destiny lies in the hands of the living God who made me.

*   *   *   *   *

Suppose a lot of old Hottentot savages who never saw a cake or tasted a cake should be selected to sit in judgment upon a baker's output. How could they discriminate as to the flavor and the quality? They might say that there was too much or too little of something that suited or displeased them, but what would their judgment amount to? It takes the test of the skillful and scientific cakemaker to determine the fault. Another thought I got out of this hypothesis is that the poor little batch of dough is not to be held responsible for its own construction. I don't know who is exactly, but that is another matter for God to take care of and settle. If some ancestor of mine put too much spice in the cake of which I am the present loaf and baking, there is one thing certain—I shall not be held responsible for the fiery flavor I had nothing to do with formulating!

Of the many things to strike the stroller on his rounds, the discriminating capacity of the average dry goods clerk calls for considerable wonderment. As I stood in one of our largest stores the other day, grasping my bundle, which, true to the type of woman's bundle-making, was loosely constructed and far from elegant, I said to myself: "Amber, do you think if these dapper counter-jumpers who draw the line so finely between the woman who carries a dog and the woman who carries a bundle, were selling loyalty by the pattern, honor and truth by the yard, purity in crystal fringes, or charity and ingenuousness by the piece, with gentle dealing and courteous speech by the card, the rush would be so great to buy? Would this haughty dame stand by so patiently if she were here to purchase a little happiness, in barter of her own, for her neighbor?" Would these patrician girls with straight profiles and untroubled eyes show the same alacrity to buy inward adornment that they manifest for outward show? To anybody of an introspective turn of mind, prone to cast his thoughts away onward into the future, to a time when false discrimination and external seeing shall vanish like last year's dandelion puffs in the first fall wind, the show of life's vain parade is a saddening spectacle after all. The superficial gloss on the manners of the sycophantic clerk, like starch in a cheap fabric; the avidity the woman displays in buying buttons and furbelows, forgetting all the time the little adornments for the robe she must wear the other side the tomb; and the cool calculation of girlish hearts that weigh gain over against good, and make no question of any profit that costs them their womanhood to attain—all this furnishes bitter reflection to sadden the heart and destroy one's faith in the adjustment of things as God created them.

Suppose one was born a Gradgrind, with a geometric heart and a castiron brain. Suppose one never saw anything but a yellow weed in a cowslip, and an accumulation of tinted vapor in a sunset. Suppose one never heard anything but running water in an April brook, and an inaccuracy of assorted notes in the song of a bobolink. In short, suppose one was born with a stomach, but with no poetic sentiment; with arms and legs, but none of those finer attributes that make of the soul a mimosa flower; what then? Why, in that case, my dear, a day like this, a storm like the splendid carnival of wind and rain last night, a fire in the grate, or a fire in the west at sunset time, a rose on its stalk, or a rose in the east at dawn, would have no more effect upon us than so much dew dropped on the back of a whale! Blessed are they who never grow too old, or too busy, or too tired to dream. Blessed be the business man who never gets to be so thoroughly a business man that he cannot take time every spring to go to Italy on a magnolia bough, as Prue's dear old bookkeeper husband did, or to visit his castles in Spain now and then, when the days are full of autumn haze and the fine dust of the golden-rod.

"I have heard it said that we have no mountains in the vicinity of Chicago," said a grizzled old Board of Trade man to me the other day. "Why, that's all wrong! We have rosier peaks and whiter summits than any Alps, and they show every clear night along the western horizon!" Wasn't that a pretty fancy for an old wheat reckoner to keep in his heart?

* * * * *

Do you think such a man will ever have his passport papers to the fair country over the border? Why, my dear, half the world, what with its money-getting passion and love of greed, won't know what to do with themselves in heaven if the grace of God

ever gets them there! They will see nothing but 95 per cent specimens in the golden
streets and a first-rate greenhouse specu-
lation in the garden of Paradise. Imagine
a latter day dollar-chaser set down suddenly
in heaven. He would be as out of place
there as a hornet in a jug of cream or a
grain reaper in a feather factory.

* * * * *

Cultivate a little more sentiment, indulge
now and then in a wholesome romance,
open the window of your soul to the east
and let the morning sun gild your ideas; it
will not harm you, and it will make you an
infinitely more pleasant companion than
you now are.

I have been thinking out some new beatitudes. The original list is getting rather
hackneyed and needs amendment.

Blessed are ye when all men shall revile
you and call you "crank," for by that em-
blem be assured of your brain power.

Blessed are ye when you find yourself in
the minority, for of such are the salt of this
earth.

Blessed are ye when by reason of clean linen and courteous manner men call you "dude," for you shall be set apart thereby from the rabble like an eagle in a barnyard.

Blessed are ye when the evil-minded shall shoot the venomous lie at you, for thereby shall ye gain the chance to outlive it, and confound the vicious.

Blessed are ye when your purse faileth, for thereby shall you be saved from bargains which end in weariness and mortification of the flesh.

Blessed are ye when people call you without policy, for so saying they count you (unwitting) among the pure in heart.

Blessed are ye when the world calls you unpopular, for to be unpopular with men is to be popular with angels.

Once, when time was young, a certain man said unto his wife, "Arise, let us go to. Let us sell our stringed instrument, yea, even our time-piece wrought of fine gold, and buy for ourselves a suburban home, where we may increase in girth as the years go by, and where, when the fullness of our days shall be accomplished, we may lay our bones in peace."

And the wife, being feather-headed by reason of her youth, answered, "Yea, verily."

And it came to pass that they sold their stringed instrument, yea, even their time-piece wrought of fine gold, and went up into the land of the Woodites and purchased unto themselves a house and lot.

And removing thereto, they were subjected to trials that frosted the head with silver and bent the upright spine.

The house, having no fence built round about its walls, was liable to the invasion of wandering beasts. At night the brain of the feather-headed was crazed and her blood curdled by the appearance of large-eyed and horned animals who gazed through the windows and butted against the casement like evil-minded goblins.

And in the pleasant days of spring, when the pale anemone blossomed and the lilac filled the air with perfume; when the blue-bird flashed athwart the gold of the young willow, and the dandelion stars were in the meadows, it chanced that the vigor of the young man waxed low by reason of hurried leapings and "mile-per-minute" laps to catch the early train.

And it came to pass that for him the varying seasons brought small delight, by reason of the fleeting nature of his observance thereof.

And the patience of the feather-headed was worn to tatters by reason of cow-bells that never ceased their jangle, and tramps that came up like the hordes of the desert, also by reason of the scarcity in the land of serving-maids.

And the two planted a garden. And they straightway laid their peas fathoms deep, so that even unto this day they came not up.

And the sprightly potato-bug took possession of the potato crop.

And the shrieks of the feather-headed rent the air by reason of the appearance of the noisome bug upon her stockings.

Likewise the advent of large green worms that moved slowly and had horns.

Now the carrot yield of that garden was immense, chiefly by reason of its undesirability.

And the spirit of the young man waxed

6

wroth, and he smote himself and talked vainly.

And the two took counsel together, saying, "Lo, we will go into the chicken business."

And the neighbors reviled the feather-headed by day so that her eyes were red with weeping, saying continually unto her: "What! and shall we scour our doorsteps and make clean the portals of our habitations that your chickens may track them again to defilement? Shall we plant flower beds for your fowls to lay waste?"

And they lifted the heel against her.

Now the nights were robbed of rest by reason of the dread of thieves who made merry in the devastation of the chicken coops.

And the early morning hours came to be a season of exceeding wrathfulness of temper, together with much profanity, on account of the wakeful rooster, who rent the dawn with the shrill clarion of his call.

Yet it came to pass that if a chicken were needed for dinner there was none in all the land to kill it.

"Indade, mum," the red-armed damsel

who ruled the kitchen would remark, "the tinder heart of me wud prevint that same."

So in time the spirit of the young man fainted within him, and his chickens became to his unquiet fancy a goblin brood that ruled the land.

And he sought forgetfulness in the great city. Yea, in the theater his soul found delight.

And it came to pass that the latter days of that young man were worse than the first, for the road on which his possessions bordered lay far back from the steam highway. So that returning homeward by night, when as yet there was no promise of dawn in the sky and the silence of death was over all the earth, the young man often stumbled by the way, bruising his flesh, rending his garments and greatly exciting his spirit.

And once as he groped his course in a darkness that might have been cut with sharp knives, behold a pallid object confronted him, and raising itself upon luminous hind legs that seemed shaped of white sea-fog, it silently waved its paws in his face, yet made no sound.

And the young man fled like a swift bird

to his dwelling-place, and finding the feath-er-headed alert and on the watch for the coming of the stealthy thief he said unto her, "Either my brain faileth me or a white kangaroo is abroad in the land."

And the fame of the white kangaroo spread mightily. So that none dared venture forth at night save with exceeding terror and knees that smote together mightily.

Moral: Think twice before sinking all that thou hast in suburban property.

What has become of the old-fashioned custom of "visiting?" I would give the world to experience again the thrill of delight that used to animate my heart when grandfather got out the old democrat wagon and we all piled in to go spend the day at a distant neighbor's. To save my life I can never experience anything but weariness with the modern formula of ceremonious calls. There is no cheer in them—they are as cold as the hearts of the society women who make them. We used to carry our knitting or our sewing and go visiting in

calico gowns, but now my lady is gloved
and laced and bonneted in the height of
style and maintains the same ceremony for
a morning call that one would expect in the
Queen's drawing-room. Heigh-ho for the
good old days when hospitality was a common virtue and formality and ostentation
were not with us; when folks went to see
each other because they were sure of a welcome, and not because they wanted to com-
pare notes as to who could make the most
display; when the dinner was spiced with
friendly chat and whatever gossip was
served with the tea was of the harmless sort,
free from scandal; when the children went
along and were not left at home with hired
girls; when everything was heartsome and
homely and cheery, and hospitality meant
greater things than a bit of pasteboard and a
stiff interchange of bloodless conventionali-
ties.

Once upon a time there was a girl. In
no respect did she differ from other girls,
save perhaps that she was a little gentler
than most. So far as a loving father or

brother counted, this dear child was without protection. The only shield between her tender heart and sorrow was a frail little widowed mother, who worked early and late to keep a certain gray wolf from the door, a gaunt and hungry creature called Want, whose scent is keen and whose fangs are cruel once fastened in the heart. The years drifted away in snow and blossom until one day the tired little mother laid her weary head upon the bosom of Death, and left the young girl desolate indeed. A few friends stood by long enough to see the grave closed over the dead, and then the girl turned to face an absolutely relentless world alone. What chance had she in a battle in which strong men grow lean of soul and broken of body? She tried to secure a place to teach, but in these days of political preferment she might as well have tried for nomination on a Presidential ticket. She drifted in and out of positions for which either her strength was inadequate or her capacity insufficient. At last, discouraged and too early spent with the attritions of a world that serves delicate and sensitive natures as the upper and nether millstones serve the wheat-kernel, the young girl dropped out of sight, and her name was heard no more in the few homes where she had been inmate or guest. This world is full of awfully selfish men and women, and every day the number grows. Each one has enough to do to keep his own head above the seething waters, and to watch over the interests of the few for whom he may be directly responsible, without taking too much concern unto himself about the fortunes of an orphaned or dowerless girl. This child of whom I write had no near relatives. The few distant kin she owned were poor and too absorbed in the riddle of life to watch over her safe solution of the same. So when she was gone nobody took the matter deeply to heart. A certain little crippled girl who peddled flowers in a corner of the depot and a poor old colored man who sold papers from the curbstone missed her for a time, and a few girl friends who had loved her mourned awhile for the sound of her voice and the sight of her sweet face, but the void soon closed and the world fared on as though this bit of wayside life had never bloomed within it.

The other day I chanced to visit a charitable institution located in a distant city. In

one of the wards of a scrupulously kept but
unhomelike place I came across a familiar
face. Wan and wasted it lay like a broken
flower upon the pillow of one of a long row
of cots. There was something about the
droop of the mouth and the glint of gold in
the brown hair of the girl who lay dying before me that recalled the gentle presence of
a long-vanished face. Inquiry elicited the
truth. The dying pauper in the charity
ward of a great institution was the girl the
brief outline of whose pathetic life is given
above. Through circumstances it was most
kind to ignore, leaving their resultant trage-
dy to one who judged more wisely and char-
itably than the stony-hearted and Pharisaical
world, the young girl had descended from
her high and fair estate to this. Left alone
in the world, too weak in body to cope with
the world's harshness, too gentle in spirit
to resist its seductions, she fell, and God in
infinite mercy thus early gathered her from
the snare of the evil-minded and the unfaithful to set her bewildered soul free in his
own good time, as the imprisoned bird
springs from the enfanglement and the
fright of capture. If only some dear, good
mother of young girls, knowing the deso-

lation of this girl when her mother left her
all alone, had opened the doorway of her
own home to the bewildered feet! It was
not charity that she needed; it was home
and a mother. It was not within the walls
of a well-managed home for working
women that she would have found security
and peace and the chance to unfold the possibilities of a very sweet and gentle nature;
she needed just such a home as yours and
mine, full of light and laughter and music
and song, with pictures and books to make
it cheerful, and love to keep it warm and
happy. There are thousands just such lonely girls out in the cold world to-night.
Mother and father are dead, no sister and no
brother to watch over them and beguile the
lonely days with bright companionship;
what wonder that they go astray and drop
out of the way, like rose leaves that flutter
in the dust at the touch of the rude wind.
Open your hearts and your homes to such
girls. For their dead mother's sake try and
be something like a mother to them. Surround them with love, watch over and counsel them along with your own girls, and for
every such deed of heavenly mercy receive

a jewel by and bye for that crown we are
going to wear throughout the eternal years.

As the years go on how full they grow to
be of ghosts. Who of us, after first youth,
have failed to find our holidays and our an-
niversaries haunted by restless memories
and sad associations that stalk like sheeted
specters from the tomb? We grow to dread
the coming of these festival days just because they are so full of the spirits of the past.
How many wish that they might lie down
and sleep through and over these holiday
times, thus banishing the thoughts that lie
away down deep in the hearts whence the
saddest tears well? "I used to anticipate
the coming of Thanksgiving and Christmas," said a friend to me the other day, "but
this year the very thought is maddening."
Why? Because the first snow of the season
fell upon her husband's grave in Rose Hill,
where barely a half-year ago she laid him
and her heart together. And when once the
ghosts get to coming into our life, oh, how
fast they throng. We cannot take a jour-

ney but they go with us. We cannot lie down to rest, or rise to take up life's multiform duties, but they lie down and rise up with us. Only at the door of death shall we leave them and enter in to find the better part of life in the shadowy land of dreams.

All day long it has been snowing, and to me not even June, with its showering appletree flowers and its alternations of silver rain and golden sunshine, is more beautiful than these soft winter days full of snow feathers and gray shadows. I love to watch the young pines take on their holiday attire. How they robe themselves from head to foot in draperies of fleecy white, pin diamonds in their dark branches, and wind about their slender girth the strands of evanescent pearl. I love to watch the skies at dawn (I should like it better if dawn came a few hours later), when they kindle like a very flame above the bluffs and scatter sparkles of light as a red rose scatters its petals. Where has the last year fled? It seems but a day's span since I sat by this same window and watched the lilac plumes yonder on that old bush in the snow bank and laughed myself sick to see the children's young kid tackle the dandelion blows. At this rate it won't be farther away than day after to-morrow morning when you and I wake up and find ourselves old folks. How odd it will be to lift our palsied members from off the couch and in a piping voice complain of the grasshopper's burden. To look in the glass and see the wisps of frosted stubble in place of the curling locks of brown and jet and gold. Ah well, it is a comfort to think that some spirits defy time and are as young at seventy as at seventeen. Beauty fades and witchery departs, but true hearts, like wine, mellow and enrich with years.

Before me lies an old book, lettered in gilt, "Leaves of Affection." The binding is frayed, the leaves somewhat dog-eared, and the general appearance of the volume indicates a rough passage. It is a school-girl's autograph collection, and the dates run back into the sixties. Nearly thirty years ago the owner of this little volume wrote in the stiff, round hand so much in vogue with the past generation, the fol-

lowing pretty sentiment on the fly-leaf of
what was then a brave new book:

> " 'Twill be sweet in after years,
> When my eyes are filled with tears,
> When my weary heart is sore
> With the woes of life's grim war,
> And my heavy spirits seek
> Solitude to think and weep,
> 'Twill be sweet indeed for me
> Then to soothe my misery
> By the words herein engraved,
> And the dear names here displayed."

The girl was very young when she wrote
these lines, and if I remember rightly had
not attained the dignity of her first long
dress. Her flaxen hair was worn in a braid,
and the bread and butter marks outnum-
bered the tear stains on her jolly round face.
As she read the lines over to the admiring
friends of the long ago time, how they
laughed together in their sleeves at thought
of any after years that should fill her eyes
with tears, of any sore heart for her, precipi-
tated by hand to hand conflict in life's "grim
war." But the years have fled away as years
have had the fashion of flying ever since
Father Time set his autograph to the calendar, and yesterday in overlooking an old
trunk away out in a peculiarly ill-kept wood-

shed, a gaunt old girl in a pink Mother Hubbard, with hair strained tight off her battle-scarred face, and no end of coal dust and smut upon her battered features, ran across this book, and sat right down on an overturned rag-bag and wept aloud at the memories that came to life with each faded leaf's turning. "Tears?" I should think there had been tears, whole rivers of them, shed for sorrows that have darkened the air like crows' pinions. "Grim war?" So much of it that from the tip of her head to the toe of her foot madam is scarred like a honeycomb, and yet, so far, she has run up no flag of truce, nor called for any quarter.

Let me see; the first name recorded brings back from the past pretty Miss Amy Sewall, the dear little teacher who used to pray with the bad girls instead of scold them, and for whom any one of us would have laid down our lives to save from sorrow.

"God forbid," writes she, "that you, dear child, be found at last outside the great garner into which angels shall shout the 'Harvest Home.'" A moment's pause for thought as this faded leaf flutters through my fingers is insufficient to decide the question as to whether the "dear child" is inside or outside the harvest car at the present writing. Perhaps her chances will fall among the gleanings which some belated harvester shall scurry up with a rake, and pitch in with the harvest after nightfall.

"Thy spirit knows that Emma loves thee," writes the next one. Poor Emma. In spite of the burden of her affection she stole my first beau away from me, and we parted next door to blows.

Here is the name of Joe Colburn. How I wish her eyes might fall upon the words I write to-night, so that she should send me a message back from the land of silence whither she drifted so long ago. The merriest madcap girl that ever sparkled a black eye beneath silken lashes or turned an ankle in a romping race. Whether she be dead or alive I know not, but even heaven will be a cheerier place to tarry in with her bright spirit as an angel comrade.

And here is jolly Hannah's faded mark. I wonder if in the corner of the world whither fate drifted her, as the current of a river floats a leaf to strand it on a stone, she ever thinks of the days when her blithe laugh rang through the old dormitory halls, .

and her peculiar bit of slang, "Git up to smash," wrought woe in the section teacher's gentle breast. Hannah was a daisy, and could I see her to-night standing before me in the pink satin bonnet that she used to wear on top of her bright brown hair, I would cheerfully forfeit a hundred dollars of the fortune that Time is bringing me in his belated boat.

"It is a glorious thing to resist temptation, but a safe thing to avoid it," wrote Hiram himself, the father confessor and head of us all. The old man has been in his grave this many a year, but if reports be true the latter part of his life was devoted to neither resisting nor avoiding. He died in the Washingtonian Home. What an old fraud he was, and how customary it is for a male preceptor of a girl's school to be a cross betweeen a rogue and a hypocrite. Hiram had a wife who used to wait upon him like a servant, and whom he used to abuse like a coward; he was all smiles to the rich girls and pickles to the poor ones. His own son used to make faces at him behind his back, and I myself told him once in one of our exciting interviews that he reminded me of Legree, in Uncle Tom's Cabin. The memory of that bit of sincerity on my part has sweetened a retrospective half-hour of my life.

Here is the autograph of Beulah Vaughan. I can hardly decipher the words, but I think the sentiment of her verse, like all the rest, breathes pure and undying affection. How Beulah used to sing when she took the tenor in the song, "There'll be no more sorrow there," just at the time for evening prayers, when the big school room was dim with shadows, and the autumn winds were harping an accompaniment in the branches of the pines that made somber the seminary grounds. It used to seem to me as though heaven was only a stone's throw away, and I would lean my head on my desk and cry to be there. Poor Beulah married early, and died young with a broken heart. Her husband put her happiness and his own pride, with both their fortunes, into a whisky glass and drained the contents. He went to prison for forgery, and she to her grave.

"Jennie Burr" is the next name recorded. She was another singer, and that is all I can remember of her, excepting a figure like a

7

willow spray, and a pair of gentle eyes that rarely smiled.

And Little Mollie—I think the child meant it when she wrote, "My darling, I have loved you from the first, and I shall love you always;" but love with some gentle little people is like the flavor of molasses candy, awfully sweet while it lasts, but soon forgotten.

"Dearest," wrote another, "May thy life ever be as calm as when the noonday sun is floating on the moonlit sea." According to subsequent developments this long-ago wish has been verified. The sublime calm of my life, so far, has been about upon a par with the cyclonic convulsions of nature that should force a noonday sun to ride a moonlit sea.

"Work on earth and rest in heaven," wrote sweet Flavia Capin. Well, I have fulfilled the first part of the injunction, Flavia dear, and am waiting for the last.

"My precious one," wrote Nettie Williams, "May the realities of thy future excel any possible anticipation." They have, Nettie. Nothing that I could have anticipated in the days when we flirted so desperately with the young man in the village

post-office could possibly have exceeded
the realities of my existence thus far.

"Integrity, fidelity and virtue adorn fe-
male character," wrote the wildest girl in
school, and the sight of the faded handwrit-
ing recalls to my mind many a mad esca-
pade we two took part in together. Wherever she may be to-night, I wonder if she
ever thinks of the post-office we had in the
old hollow-tree, and the ardent love-letters
we exchanged there with callow village
youths. I wonder if she ever stops to smile
as I do to recall our foragings for provender
when the store-room was locked for the
night, and the billet of dried beef we cherished all term-time so tenderly, spoiling
many a good eraser in chipping nutriment
from its granite sides.

Ah, well, one cannot sit forever on an
overturned rag-bag and weep over the days
that are no more. So the woman closed the
old book with a sigh, and took up the toma-
hawk again to charge upon the realities of
a prosaic present.

"It is of no use!" cried I, flinging my pencil at a far "too previous" blue-bottle fly

which had insisted upon taking my nose for
an early blossom until patience went to
windward like a spume of foam in a gale;
"it is of no use; a dog-day has dropped
down in April, and I shall vanish before it
like stubble in a flame! What can I do to
keep cool?"

"Drink pepper tea," said one whose suggestions are always maddening.

"Keep calm," said another whose wisdom
transcends his years.

"I'll take a ride on the cable-car, forward
seat!" said I, and started.

As usual, when I signaled the car the
driver mistook me for a merry lunatic whil-
ing the time away in harmless sport. He
didn't pretend to stop his car, although I
hailed it from the upper crossing of an in-
tersecting street, according to orders. Finally, becoming excited, I charged down
the track like an Indian brave on the warpath, and when with a flying leap I boarded
the car I had hardly breath left to give
thanks.

I wish I knew what it all means. I wonder what they really think a woman intends
when she stands on a street corner with her
hand uplifted like a village church-spire, or

waves her arm like a banner, or skips to and fro like a playful lamb. I wonder what they think she really has upon her mind when she chases the car for a whole block, and bursts into tears when she fails to over-take it. I wonder what they believe to be the reason of her excitement when she cries "Ah, there! Stop your old car, can't you?" Evidently there is a misapprehension some-where. Either the car means to boycott the women, or we have not struck upon the ap-propriate signal for their detention. Some day I shall buy me an air-gun (after the blessed pony is paid for), and I shall take my stand on the legitimate crossing, and when the drivers fail to stop at my command, one by one they shall fall as withered leaves fall in a frost, and as noiselessly. Nobody will know that I and my little air-gun personate the deadly frost; but as time goes on and the mortality among drivers becomes alarming there will be a rumor in the town that it will be healthier to stop the car when a woman signals it.

Let me say right here that I know of no better cure for nervousness than a ride on the front seat of a grip on a bright day. No dread of being run away with; no sympathy expended on overworked and overheated horses; no fear but what in event of a collision, the grip will get the best of it. A breeze like the wind that freshens a sail, direct in your face; the hum of the cable to accentuate your delight, as the ring of the iron rails behind a flying train will set the pulses beating. To be sure the advance is a little jerky, something like that of a Kansas grasshopper, but you soon get used to that.

At my right hand to-day sat two bright-eyed girls eating peanuts. The way they bit into the crackling shells, nibbled out the kernels, and munched steadily away, set me thinking of a couple of full-cheeked squirrels up in a tree-top. The trace, however faint, is undisputed that links us with the animal kingdom. Whether it appears in a feature, an expression, or a habit like this eating of peanuts and chewing of gum in public places, it never fails to provide the gossamer link that binds us to the pre-historic globule.

At my left sat a type of the great unwashed. The wind blew off shore or I should have killed myself. There was something about him that made me remember a piece of Limburger cheese which the Doctor once put inside my handkerchief box. That was long ago, and the boy who did the deed is now in better business, but its memory returns to me on occasions such as these.

Near me sat a young girl with a face which reminded me of an andante movement in one of Beethoven's symphonies, or of an evening sky before the stars have found it. There was such veiled strength and beautiful possibility in it, that speaking to her with the voice of my soul I said, "You delightfully natural, a trifle prim, but altogether lovely girl! Why are there not more of your kind nowadays? No bangs, no choker collars, no airs, no mannerisms. A smooth brow, a dainty ruffle, thorough repose of manner, and quiet dignity mark you a type as distinct from the average Chicago girl as a primrose in a garden of weeds. To meet you is like coming across a bunch of genuine sweet-peas in a milliner's stock of muslin posies!"

A colored woman with a silhouette baby dressed in the regulation costume that has served to make our own babies so bewitching of late, took her seat among the many

who rode with me. That baby was about
the cunningest thing I ever saw. Its eyes
were black as jet beads, its hair a shade or
so darker, and its complexion at least three
tints blacker still. It was solemnly sucking
a large stick of striped candy, the one color
in a carnival of gloom. A white baby is
angelic, but a black baby is simply adorable.
I should like one around for recreation
when I get the blues. Anybody who could
see it roll its eyes and purse its mouth, like
a diminutive raven contemplating death,
the tomb and eternity, and not laugh, was
born without the power of appreciating the
humorous aspects of life.

The man whom I long to bid God-speed
to Joliet occupied a seat near me, and almost washed me out of the car with a freshet
of tobacco juice. Oh how I shall smite the
cymbal and beat the drum when that man
goes into stripes! And the time is coming.
Out there in Kansas the other day, they ran
an entire woman ticket right through to
victory. If the new Mayor of that Western
hamlet is anything like me, she will come
down upon the tobacco spitting fiend like
the Assyrian on the fold. By the ear she
will march him off to prison, there to linger

in durance vile until all the seas he has let loose to pollute woman's skirts "gang dry," and into his disreputable tabernacle of flesh and blood the good Lord shall flash the reflection of decency and good manners. I hate him so, my dear, that the violence of my emotion must excuse the sharpness of my temper when I write of him.

When at last I alighted from the car, after riding eight miles through scenes as varying as life in a great cosmopolitan city can furnish, I was as cool and happy as if I had been bowling along the boulevard in Mrs. Lofty's carriage, behind her sleek and handsome grays. For it is not what we have, so much, that yields us joy in life as how we take it. If one used a harp only as a fire-screen, we should never know what heavenly sounds were held captive by its strings. It is the way we use our harps, as well as our opportunities, that brings out the music in them.

"Do you really believe," asked a pretty girl of me the other day, "that any woman ever actually died because the man she loved was cruel?"

My dear child, to answer that question I should have to begin with Eve, who, I have no doubt, drooped and faded from the time that Adam told tales about her, and follow all along the line to where the poor little girl died in the hospital the other day because her lover deserted her, and even then I should be no more certain than I was when I started along the shadowy list. The ethics of this passionate human heart of ours are past all finding out. They cannot be discussed lightly, nor can a woman who never had a headache catalogue the symptoms and progress of other folk's pericardic disturbances. I do not believe that a sick soul has symptoms that can be diagnosed. You can study out and prescribe for a bilious disturbance, but there is no skill this side the wisdom of heaven that can minister to a mind diseased. When an apple is stung by a venomous insect it simply shrivels up, drops from the bough and dies. So with the heart stung with ingratitude or contempt; it loosens its hold on life and drops. You may call it heart-break if you like, but the processes are past finding out.

CHAPTER III.

A FAIRY STORY FOR GROWN UP PEOPLE.

A fairy once grew discontented with Fairyland. Strange that a dainty being fed on butterfly-steaks and rose-leaf pudding, whipped dew and cobweb cake, should ever tire of the cuisine, and grumble at the fare. But this little Elf of whom I write did certainly grow weary of them all, and long for a change of scene and climate. Perhaps his nerves asserted themselves as they sometimes do with grosser mortals, and he suffered from neuralgia; or his cobweb cake had too much ozone in it and caused dyspepsia. If so, who of us can blame him for growing whimsical and hard to suit? So the little fellow applied for leave of absence.

"Where would you choose to go?" asked the Queen after listening to his petition, thoughtfully stroking her nose the while with the section of a violet leaf, as was her custom when perplexed.

"I should like to visit Chicago, the city by the great lake in which no fairy has ever set foot through all the years of its magical growth. I would like to see for myself how mortals live and prosper who make their gold from pork, ride without horses, and manufacture moonlight by electricity."

"It is a somewhat dangerous undertaking you contemplate," replied the Queen. "Have you reflected upon the risks to be run by an organization like yours, which has never known a fiercer alarm than the buzz of the mosquito or the ripple of wind-stirred leaves; which has never strayed beyond these quiet forest-glades, or soared higher than the turret of the lily bell, or the lattice of the rich red rose? How will you endure so long a flight and so mighty a transformation of scene and surroundings?"

"I have pondered long and earnestly upon it all," replied the Elf, "and desire grows ever stronger within my breast to fly away and visit the great city of my dreams."

"Then be it even as you wish," said the Queen, uplifting, as she spoke, a crimson trumpet flower and winding a long and mellow note which quickly summoned her attendant courtiers to her side. "See to it," said she, addressing her high chamberlain, a gorgeous personage dressed in a pansy leaf doublet and hose of daffodil-yellow, "that this noble Elf has transportation by the first Nautilus steamer sailing from port, with choice of state room and reserved seat at the Captain's table. I send you by water route," continued she, turning to the delighted Elf and laying her finger softly against her wine-red lip, "because the new law has not affected marine passes, and the royal treasury is just now very low."

When the Elf found himself, after an eventful passage, alone in the mighty city, his delight knew no bounds. The roar of countless mingled noises resolved itself into a mighty diapason of melodious sound, that seemed to him grander than any wind among the pines, or thunders of the north. The sight of children leaping in the sun, (for it was summer time and Michigan Boulevard was full of little ones and their nurses) filled his heart with joy, and he ran to join them. But no one noticed his salutation, nor seemed in the least affected by his demonstrations of good-fellowship. One little golden-headed baby, seated like a young Princess within a chariot of silver and blue, threw out her hands and laughed as he approached, but was wheeled swiftly by, and he was left alone.

"Strange;" he mused; "can it be that these grand and glorious mortals are blind, that their beautiful eyes see me not?"

So after awhile he tucked his wings under him and nestled into a corner to watch and meditate.

Now be it known that all super-natural beings, be they fairies or angels, are endowed with double sight; the eyes that see the external, and the more wonderful eyes which look through externals at the heart and life. So it came to pass that the Elf was witness to many wonderful things, and being quick of wit and unfettered by any material biases toward wealth values and social ambitions, he very soon put two and two together and came to an understanding of the problem. He noticed that there was something which made many the recipients of universal homage, while others walked the streets unnoticed and without the bestowal of smile or lifted hat from any who passed them by. He saw plainly dressed young girls, and delicate, tired-looking women whose souls within their breasts were like singing birds or blowing lilies, and yet they walked apart and gained no meed of courtesy or love. He saw men within whose breast a snake was coiled, or a wild beast crouched, and the way before them was like the advance of a king through fawning courtiers. Everybody bowed to the ground and did them homage. He saw women clad in velvets and decked with jewels, and within their breasts was nothingness and within their heads were feathers, and yet they walked with high heads, and the passers-by made way before them.

"It is dress which makes the difference," quoth the Elf to himself after awhile. "It is not the man or the woman which commands the mortal world's respect, but the garments in which they clothe themselves."

So, being vested with much power, and with a roguish nature withal, the Elf conceived a plan to while away the time, for the bustle of a big city had tired him and he was getting a little weary of it all.

"I will reverse things for an hour," said he, "and see what will happen when mortals see each other as they are, and know each other as the fairies know them."

Accordingly he drew a circle about him, and sat him down once more to view the sport. The first to enter the charmed ring was a slip of a girl in a cotton gown, and clasping to her breast a picture of anemones and violets which she had toiled to paint, and was trying to sell that she might buy wine and fruit for a dying mother. As she stepped within the enchanted circle, lo! her cotton gown changed to lustrous satin, pure as a lily's leaf, and on her soft brown hair fell the shadow of a golden crown. The pictured flowers she carried became genuine blossoms, and seemed to have their roots within her heart. Amazed, the people who saw the transformation rushed to give her greeting as a strange and royal Princess whom they delighted to know, but she was borne swiftly away out of their sight in a cloud of snowy whiteness.

The next who came within the magic ring was a portly woman with a double chin, and two big red ears weighted down with diamonds. Accompanying her were her maiden daughters robed in silk of Parisian make and texture, and with ruby-throated humming-birds upon their bonnets. No sooner had the trio stepped within the elfin circle than the haughty dame took. on the outward semblance of a scrub-woman clothed in filthy rags; her diamonds changed to tear drops wrung from the hearts she had unjustly dealt with, and her shoes gaped full of holes. Her pretty daughters were changed to kitchen wenches clothed in grease and ashes, and on their heads, where erst the murdered bird had drooped its bright wings, was a ghastly toad and a strangled mouse! The commotion caused by this terrible transformation scene, as the crowds shrank back with groans and cries, was too great to admit of further tarrying on the part of the somewhat frightened Elf. So he spread his wings and flew away, whither, I have not yet been able to learn, that I might follow.

The other day the eternal silence gathered to itself, softly as a brooding cloud summons a mist from the mountains, a tender wife and mother. I wish I could tell you how beautiful the funeral services were that consigned what was left of that beau-

tiful personality to the keeping of the resurrection angel! Although I cannot do that,
by reason of the sacredness of a grief which
longs to keep its dead from public mention,
I can use the memory of this beautiful
service to point a moral and adorn a tale.
What spectacle is more revolting to good
taste and delicate instincts than the formula
of a modernly conducted funeral? The procession of curious strangers who file about
the coffin! The eye askance at the adornment of the dead. The neighbor who drops
in to see the show as she would attend a
circus were the admission free. The casual
onlooker who counts the rows of crape on
the widow's skirt and the poor thing's sobs
all in the same breath.

A poor man's funeral is apt to be nothing
but a ghastly parade, expensive from first
to last. "Shure we'll give him a rousin'
funeral," says honest Paddy, and the expense incurred would have kept his widow's
bin in coal for a year. The living are made
to suffer that the unheeding dead may go
to their grave with a big demonstration.
If the wealthier classes would simplify these
final services more and more the effect for
good upon the poorer classes would be in-

calculable. As long as time endures the poor will imitate the rich. Let the lesson set them, then, be wholesome and as sensible as possible. May some of us live to see the dawn of a new order of things; to see funerals become less pretentious and more holy; less of a ceremony and more of a sacrament. To see grief off parade; to see more tenderness shown the living, and less of ostentation displayed when it is too late to be of any comfort. Fewer roses held in dead hands and more buds clasped in living fingers. This would be a welcome sight, I think, in the eyes of heaven and the angels.

Next to a match that won't light is a friend who won't stand up for you in an emergency. There are lots of friends for every one of us who are always ready to say a good word for us when we don't need it, but when the time comes to test them they fly away like birds at the approach of the cat. I humbly hope that in the next world, if not in this, we shall have a better chance to find out what true, unalterable, unscarable, and perfect loyalty is. I should like to spend my first few centuries in heaven in the enjoyment of such friendship as I have dreamed of here. A friendship that cares not one straw whether you are poor and illy-clothed or rich and arrayed in purple vestments. A friendship that, so long as your soul is clean and true, don't care a fig how much money you make or how successful you are, but casts its lot with yours whether you munch crusts or feed on pheasants. A friendship that will walk alongside whether you walk on cobble stones or ride in a carriage over the king's highway. Yes, my dear, that experience will be quite blissful enough to occupy a few centuries without taking up immediate harp practice or joining in the grand hallelujahs!

I would rather visit an old grave-yard any day than go listen to the finest sermon that was ever preached. I can get nearer heaven on a tomb-stone than by any other method yet tested. So, when somebody said to me in Portland the other day, "Why don't you go up on the East Hill and visit the old burying-ground?" I jumped at the chance as some folks would to hear Paderewski play or Spurgeon preach.

It was a lovely morning, and Portland City shone like a newly-swept and garnished parlor after cleaning day. There was not a rose in any one of the pretty side-yards of the town that did not wear a pink bonnet pinned with a dew-drop stick-pin, and not a clematis-vine or a woodbine anywhere that did not look as though newly curled and scented like a dude fresh from a barber shop.

"Did you ever see a prettier city?" asked the man who was carrying the lunch-basket and the umbrellas, to say nothing of the shawl-strap and the novels.

"It is indeed a beautiful place," answered I, "but I think half of its beauty comes by comparison. If one had never seen a flower one would be prone to magnify the charm of even a wayside blossom. It is because we have lived in the dirtiest, noisiest and most unattractive city in the world so long that Portland seems like a marvel of loveliness to us."

"That may be true to a degree," said the man with the burden, "but, outside of any comparison, I think the Union does not hold a cleaner, sweeter or more delightfully-situated city than this seaport town."

By this time we had climbed the hill and stood spell-bound on the crest that swept the whole country-side, from the blue sea on the East to the bluer mountains that hovered like sapphire clouds in the West. Meadow lands snow-white with daisies drifted between, and soft bosomed lakes ruffled by crimpling winds spread at our feet. Far away the farmers were harvesting hay, and the landscape was dotted with dimpling hills that freighted each puff of wind with a sweetness born of sunshine and shower. The picture was so inconceivably lovely that we stood long before it, unmindful of passing time.

"Just think of the view one gets from any standpoint that sweeps Chicago!" said I. "For these blue lakes we get the Chicago River, an abomination to both sight and smell; for these lovely meadow lands and rolling hills we get Bridgeport, the Stock Yards and miles upon miles of dumping-ground and unattractive suburb; and in place of the limitless blue of the Atlantic we are forced to be content with an area of unsalted waterway, beautiful to be sure, but painfully inadequate to one who was born and brought up by the sea."

"I don't like to hear you run down Chicago so," remonstrated the man upon whom the many bundles acted as an anchor to hold him steady before the wind. "Chicago is a grand city, and can beat the world for activity and growth; its match is not to be found on either continent."

"A bull is active when he is chasing a man across-country, and a tumor is possessed of the attribute of growth. There are better things than either, to my manner of thinking," said I. "At the same time," I continued, while we reluctantly turned our backs upon the picture we had been admiring, "I am willing to grant you that Chicago is a splendid town. Its superlative architecture and magnificent resources amaze even its severest critics, and the world cannot produce a grander exhibition of pluck and energy than the culmination of the Columbian exhibit, but somehow, even while I admire, I am reminded of the old missionary hymn which contains this couplet:

'Where every prospect pleases,
And only man is vile.'

"Take Chicago without seven-eighths of its people and I glory in it, but the finest vase in the world, if it holds soiled water, is not a desirable ornament for a fastidious woman's center-table. The past few years have attracted a set of people to Chicago from all over the world who cannot make even splendid architecture and superb achievement go down. A pill may be molded like a violet and inclosed in a sugar capsule, but neither shaping nor covering can make it other than a pill and hard to swallow."

By this time we had come to a little brown gate that led from the quiet street into a quieter one that was tangled all over with neglected rose-bushes and buttercups grown tired of holding up their goblets to the sun. There were marble doorways to every house within this little street, but they were all tight-closed, and only a few drowsy honey-bees were abroad as we stepped within the inclosure. A sweeter bit of earth wherein to seek rest was never granted to the weary dead. I hope that when my time comes to unloose the shoes from off my pilgrim feet I may find as comfortable quarters for my final bed-chamber. I want just such bowery bushes to hedge me in, and I want just such crowds of daisies to start a colony beneath the "windowless palace"

where I dream the idle years away. I want
the children to come and search for wild
strawberries just as they do every hour of
the June weather on Portland Hill, and I
want the same sleepy bird to sing a dozen
times a day while the sunlight showers its
golden dust upon the green roof of my
home.

For more than an hour we walked on together through the grassy lanes of the dear
old grave-yard. We knelt and parted the
blossoms from many a head-stone, and read
the legend of many a young life gone early
home to God. In one sunny corner we
found a patch of baby graves. It seemed
almost like a flower-bed from which the little souls were blossoming one by one.
While we watched, a shy wood-rose just
opening was "baby May;" a morning-glory's
cup, half weighted with a milk-white moth,
was "baby Jean;" a tuft of tangled forget-
me-nots held the wondering eyes of a third,
and a shred of delicate fern was the wind-
blown hair brushed back from the cherub
brow of the last of all. Upon a weather-
beaten, moss-grown stone we read of "Marjory Thorndike, aged 16," whose spirit took
up its abode with the holy angels while her

sweet body was laid aside in the dark wardrobe of the grave just fifty years ago. Was she very pretty, I wonder, and did her bright eyes close suddenly upon this glad life, or did she pine and fade slowly, like a blossom with a blight in its folded bud? Were there many left to mourn for Marjory, or was she the only child of some widowed mother who followed her light feet down to the door of the grave soon after? Many of these mounds in Portland churchyard are built above the bones of soldier boys. The records tell of scores of brave lads under twenty-five who died in various prisons or were sent home from cruel battlefields. A rain-washed flag floats over their graves, and the tears of many such tramps as the man with the bundles and I fall often upon them. I was not ashamed of the tears, nor was I ashamed that I let loose a prayer, as Indians do a bird, above every headstone that marked a soldier's resting place.

Under a lilac tree within whose ancient branches the robins built their nests we found an old, old grave, the inscription upon which went straight to the heart. "Be kind to each other: Mother," it said. I imagined a noisy household of quarrelsome

boys and girls who fought and fussed like
jackdaws. No doubt they loved each other
well enough—they always do, these squab-
blers—but they had poor ways of showing
it, and the pale little mother could never
make herself heard nor felt in the noisy
household. Nobody minded her or heeded
her gentle admonitions. Finally she died,
as tired-out mothers sometimes do, and,
stricken by a late remorse, her repentant
children inscribed one of her unheeded pre-
cepts upon the tomb-stone and entered into
a compact to be kind when it was too late to
cheer her gentle heart with any such re-
solve. I hope that every time they come to
this hill-side village, so quaint and old and
sweet, they look at "mother's" admonishing
words and enter anew upon a compact they
shall not break. But where am I? Time is
up, and still in the grave-yard! Next letter
I shall have something to tell you of a new
Paradise and the flaming sword which drove
me from it.

I took a long walk the other day, and in
the course of my ramblings, which, part of
the way lay through woods, and part of the

way by the side of birch-crowned bluffs that overlooked the sparkling waters of the big lake, I met only one thoroughly wretched-looking object, and that was a man. I came across lots of sheep, and a few cows, with here and there a busy colony of chickens, and one particularly jolly pig, but every animate thing looked care-free and happy, except the man! His hair was grizzled and thin, his countenance cadaverous and wan, and the furrows on his cheek were like the wheel-ruts on a much-traveled road. And why? Perhaps, thought I, because he had the power of imparting and making interchange of his troubles by means of the gift of speech. Who ever heard of a wrinkled-faced cow, and yet cows grow old as well as men. Who ever saw a sheep with tear-bleared eyes, and a wan and sunken face? If sheep could meet together and talk of their ailments, as we do, and fill the hours of a morning call with details of a bad digestion, the complaints the blessed children fall heir to, and the horrors of the domestic question, perhaps sheep would grow old and wizened before their time. as women do. What is mankind's universal form of salutation? "How are you?" That's the

first question we put to each other when we
meet in the morning, or after a separation,
and ten to one this question launches a full-
rigged craft of human misery upon the tide
of conversation that should be devoted to
nobler converse. The Turks approach the
subject more directly with the salutation,
"How are your bowels?" But although we
couch our sentiments in more ambiguous
language, the result is the same. How
would it do to change the form of inquiry
to matters pertaining to the spirit rather
than to the body? How is it with your soul?
Are you happy? How goes the morning,
or the day? Would not any of those saluta-
tions be better than a greeting that plunges
at once into the condition of the liver, headaches, catarrhs and hay fever? Try it.

And then when a trouble overtakes us,
be it little or big, we never go off by ourselves as the stricken deer does, or the dog
with a thorn in his foot, but we call our
neighbors and friends together, or we put
on our things and run down to mother's to
talk it over and extract all the gall there is
from the tribulation. Now it is all right
when great griefs overtake us to seek human sympathy; without it this world would

be like a desert land without an oasis, or
without a rainy shadow betwixt us and the
glaring, scorching sun. But half the little
hurts of life it were nobler and more heroic
to bear alone. If you need to take a particularly nasty dose of medicine, is it worth
while to force every member of the family
to share the dose, or to run around and com-
pel all your acquaintances to taste also?
Castor-oil and family troubles are far better
taken in individual doses, and not adminis-
tered on the communistic plan.

Another misery that would be spared us
were speech denied us, and from which
dumb animals are forever shielded, is the
excruciating torment of having to talk when
one has nothing to say. Have you not
been there all of you? Seated tete-a-tete to
a man or a woman at a lunch or on a picnic
excursion, with whom it was as difficult to
start a conversation as to raise bangs on a
billiard-ball. How you struggle inwardly,
and writhe in the throes of an attempt to
start a topic! How you cast about for a
witty remark to make that cast-iron countenance relax, or a pathetic story to bring
moisture to those fish eyes! Such agony
leaves its trace on heart and brain, and it is

purely the gift of human speech. A flock
.of sheep on a summer day lay out in the
clover, nibble at the sorrel, chew the cud
of happy fancy and are supremely happy
without the interchange of a single sound.
But a flock of men and women turned loose
in a parlor for an evening party! Of what
do they talk? With a babble of words, what
do they say? Anything worth remembering? Anything uplifting? Anything helpful and strong? For anything that an angel
might stop to jot down in his commonplace
book they might far better be dumb sheep.
There is nothing so inane under the sun as
the conversation of people who have no
ideas. The froth of whipped eggs is a tonic
compared to it. I would rather spend my
life with the cattle upon the hills and the
sheep in the fold, than put in a year with a
brainless, idealess woman, or a society dude.
Silence is heaven sent and born of eternal
wisdom compared to the crackling of a fool's
laughter and the braying of a fool's conversation. From both, dear Lord, deliver us!

A well-meaning friend sent me four hens
and a rooster the other day, because, as he

said, he was going to town to live, and thought perhaps I would enjoy keeping a few fowls. I am not the kind of woman to keep chickens. I am not sufficiently chastened. I cannot restrain the impulse to throw things at them when, looking out of the window, I behold them at this moment roosting on a tree instead of in the lordly mansion prepared for them. They are nearly frozen. There is a spark of vitality left, perhaps, in the Leghorn, but I think the rooster and the Brahmas have been dead for days. I tried to hire a boy to climb up the tree and fetch them down, but he seemed to think the offer I made him of a quarter for the job entirely inadequate. Ah, well! to-morrow morning I shall go out with a pole and dislodge them from the branches of the tree, as a happy child knocks down apples. And the fowls will not be dead after all, but with demoniac cries they will elude me and enter the domains of my next-door neighbor. And the dog will join in the chase, until the sport shall wax so deadly that I shall go in search of the friend who has thus embittered my days and cleave his hemlet with a hatchet.

I know what mighty culminations are evolved from chicken-keeping. I have alienated life-long friends, shattered the intimacies of years, and brought down upon myself the seven vials of wrath too often in the past not to know what lies in store for me if my brood of chickens multiply and come forth to possess the land. By and by there will be a holy terror of a game-cock hatched, and he will depopulate the country round about of feathered bipeds. Complaints will be made, and there will be the wild alarm of shot-guns around my peaceful dwelling, as enraged poultry-owners from far and near bear down upon my fighting rooster.

And later on my neighbor will cultivate flower-beds and tender vegetables, and I shall hire boys to watch these goblin fowls by day, that they molest not the garden beds, until my bank account dwindles to a memory and my credit becomes a by-gone dream. And I shall buy all my eggs, save one or two a week which the weasels and the rats spare me from out my own hen-house.

And when our stomachs yearn for chicken-meat there shall be no one in all the household who will dare behead a fowl. I shall try it, perhaps, and feel like first cousin to Cain ever after, although my deed will be but a futile attempt. And finally, impoverished, nervously prostrated, a mere wreck, I shall give every chicken away and tread the earth a "free man" once more, by reason of the removal of their "shadow from my door and their beak from out my heart forever." Take my advice, my dear, and when a friend says chicken to you next, go get a shot-gun, point it at him, and leave the issue to his own discretion.

How the pawn-shops are filling up this jolly winter weather. Stand before any one of them, and see how like the maws of wolves they fatten on man's misfortune. There, in one corner, hangs a string of coral beads. They clasped a baby's dimpled throat once, perhaps, but the baby grew cold and hungry for something better than crusts and away she flew to heaven. Don't you believe it hurt the mother to bring those beads and pawn them for money to buy a basket of coal?

And there is a guitar, tied with a bow of faded ribbon. What are the fingers doing now, I wonder, that once picked out dainty tunes from these strings, and where sounds the voice that filled the pretty home parlor with its melody in those bright days before hard times came knocking at the door? Before the window stands a blue and shivering wretch, and in his hand he holds—what? A bit of a looking-glass, framed in antique silver. No wonder he doesn't care to keep a mirror to reflect such bloated features. The eyes that would look back at him from its depths are not the eyes that were lifted from his crib long years ago to meet a mother's morning kiss! Away with the useless thing then! It will bring enough to purchase a hot toddy and forgetfulness, surely.

See the rings hanging on the hooks. Not one of them but could tell a tale that would harrow your comfort-taking soul. Wedding rings bartered for merely enough money to buy a six-penny loaf. And yet, when those little yellow circlets of gold went on, they stood for deathless hope, and an eternity of love! Engagement jewels, pawned from dire necessity, and never to be reclaimed by the poor, heartbroken women bankrupt of happiness long before they were of trust.   But it strikes me we are getting too near the seamy side of things.   Let us call a halt and say good-night.

It is not the worst thing in the world to be called a crank.   I find as I go about the earth that whenever a man is found with individuality enough to take a stand against being nothing more than a conformist he is a crank.   Wherever a woman is found who thinks more of her brain than of the hat which surmounts it, she is a crank. Wherever a man is found who believes he was made for some other purpose than to walk shoulder to shoulder with the "great alike," as a convict in stripes keeps step with his comrade, he is a crank.   Whereever a young girl is found who is fonder of frolic than of fashion, of her friends than of their reputation, who will stand by her lover through a prison record and the other side of prison bars, she is a crank.   Reformists are all cranks.   Discoverers are cranks. Philanthropists and poets are cranks. John Howard would be a sad crank to-day did he carry the whiteness of his life through dungeon cells to reform them. Christopher Columbus, Robert Fulton, Watts, the discoverer of steam, were horrible cranks, as viewed from to-day's standpoint. Bergh, who has done more than any other living man to lighten brute suffering, is a crank.

Please, when I die, dear friends, carve simply on my tombstone, "Amber, a Crank."

"Have you seen the tulips yet?" asked the Young Person the other morning.

"I have not," said I, and promised forthwith that I would take the first opportunity to go out and see the wonderful lake shore beds. But I knew well enough that I should never behold them in their splendor, as she had done. And why? Because it is a very different thing, my dear, to visit beds of tulips all alone by yourself on the shady side of your years, afoot, and wearily holding your skirts from the dirt; grasping a bundle and dragging a superfluous umbrella by the hair of its head, from what it is to visit them under the banner of youth, with a gay cavalier at your side, and the sound of your own laughter to fill the gaps of idle speech with music.

It creates a very different atmosphere through which to view anything this side of heaven (especially twilight and tulips), whether your age be 16 or 76; whether you ride in a cart behind a thoroughbred or trudge on your own tired feet with a twinge of rheumatics in your left ankle; or whether you be newly in love, or long since surfeited with the brimstone and honey of that erratic passion.

* * * * *

Was ever a bluer day than that which folded the lake in its soft embrace the time we really saw the tulip beds? Was ever a battle so closely drawn as that between the haze in the air and the new foliage on the trees? Was ever a world so blithe and beauty laden, reeled, sparkling, from the spinning wheel of May? Upon the velvet lawn the trees cast fleeting shadows, as girls who dance to and fro before a mirror leave reflections of their loveliness therein.

And the tulips! Imagine all the beautiful women you have ever seen or known, drawn up in ball dress array to dance a minuet. Imagine a fleet of sunset clouds adrift before the wind. Imagine God's thoughts made manifest in beauty so boundless. So free, so all-pervading that even the most worthless, sin-scarred and battle-wrecked of all humanity was welcome to draw near and bask in the sight.

There is a wee little cat, black as Satan, which every day comes out of a court window near to where I write and watches with unblinking desire a fluff of canary feathers and song that hops within a cage not far away. Only a yard or so of space separates the bird from the cat, and if tireless persistence and unwavering desire ever accomplished anything in this world, the taste of canary bird meat is going to become an established fact to puss very soon. Somehow the long continued strain of the thing is making me nervous. It is like seeing Othello always standing with the fatal pillow poised above poor Desdemona's head, or the horrid old uncle watching from behind a tree the pretty babes at play, plotting their desertion in the woods and their sad and cruel doom of death. I should like to draw a parallel right here between the cat and the "masher," the bird and the silly girl who encourages his advances. But what is the use? As long as the old earth spins, and man grinds at the wheel; as long as the sun urges his golden car through the dusty highway of the stars, men and women will be fools, and the grave will prove the only refuge from the cruelty of the one and the folly of the other. You might as well stand by a pasture fence and tell a young colt not to frisk, or look up into a hawthorn tree and tell a bird not to build its nest among the blossoms as to try and regulate the hearts of men, or dictate the caprices of women.

A robin was singing under my window this morning. I spied him there while I was dressing, and watched him so long that I missed my train. But his song was worth the lost hour. How he fluttered, and

cocked his smooth, brown head and actually winked before he began! His breast
shone in the sunshine like a mellow peach,
or like a bit of sunset cloud fallen earthward. His bright eyes glanced hither and
yon, watchful, saucy, alert for interruptions.
Suddenly he gurgled a few delicious opening notes. Then he discoursed with some
severity upon the deceitful qualities of
March, and the general unsatisfactoriness
of early sunshine. He told me confidential-
ly, of a discovery he had made of fresh
hypatica leaves in the woods, and of a sudden sortie of grass dragoons along the loosened water courses. He mentioned his ex-
pectations for April, and how he had an eye
on a corner lot in our southerly woodbine
for building purposes. Oh, how golden
sweet his song became when he trilled his
hopes as to the successful wooing of little
Miss Redbreast, although he contrived to
let me know, in a roundelay aside, he found
the young person rather feather-headed and
hard to win. Domestic duties, however,
he chirped, would settle her down soon
enough. He laughed a little self-con-
sciously as he pictured a home atilt in the
blossoms, and asked me with some concern

and a burst of lullaby notes, if I really thought that early worms were too rich a diet for very young birds. He sparkled into delicious romanzas, and mellowed into soft cadenzas; the stir of spring, the breeze of the hills, the breath of arbutus, the patter of April rain, the promise of violets, the dip of songful water, all sounded in the song he sang me, and when he spread his wings and tilted away I kissed the Young Person and vowed the world was a dear, delightful place to live in, after all, despite the trials of moving time, and house hunting—so let's be jolly, dear—let's be jolly while robins sing, and spring is on the way!

A few hours more and Sunday will again be with us. How differently the day is passed in our homes from what it used to be. In my childhood it was ushered in by dreadful preparatory scrubbings, during which the nurse polished off my face with a big crash towel and assured me that however much "good little gells" cried on weekdays, they were never known under the most harrowing circumstances to shed a tear on Sunday, that is if they cherished the faintest hope of going to heaven when they died. I always attended "divine service" as it was called, although why the gathering together to sing songs of One we love, and say all the good things about Him we could, should be called "service," was even then a conundrum to my infant brain. Caraway seeds and peppermint-drops were supplied to keep me from slumber during the long dry sermon. I remember that I wore blue shoes at that early stage of my existence, and I can even now recall how tired I used to get stretching them out to match them with the blue places in the sky which I could see through the window. We always remained through intermission to attend Sunday school. A harrowing stroll through the grave-yard took up the noon hour, and then came infant class, presided over by a grizzly old sister in the church who loved to curdle our baby blood with allusions to the "worm that never died" and the lake that seethed with "fire and brimstone." After those exhilarating services, came another long sermon for which even unlimited peppermint-drops offered no alleviation.

Then came a ride home during which my feeble intellect was taxed to remember text and topics. Then a cold dinner and an afternoon of Bible reading and verse memorizing. No music enlivened the day, no romps or out of door frolics were allowed; so that long before the years of discrimination, I came to regard Sunday as the one jet bead strung with the other six pearls of the week's calendar.

How glorious the change from the old bigotries and superstitions of the past. Gone forever the idea that He who sent little children, and birds, and bonnie blue weather into the world is content that we gather nothing but withered garlands and dead leaves. As well pick sagebrush when roses are blowing, or sit down cellar when all the shining outside world is ours, as seek to maintain the Sabbath with the old-time restrictions and limitations. Draw a big black line at the theater door, taboo minstrel melodies and noisy sports, but let us have a Sunday such as I hope we shall spend ten thousand times ten thousand together up in heaven, full of peace and loving thoughts, cheer and sunshine, helpful deeds for one another, earnest strivings

God-ward, heavenward and humankind-
ward.

There was a little friend closely inter-
woven with my life long ago, when time
(for me) was young, whose memory comes
back to me with each radiant return of
spring, and of whom I have a fancy to talk
to you to-night.

As I remember her, the child was an in-
nocent-faced little thing, with wide eyes of
golden brown, shaded by soft lashes, and
a head closely covered with a feathery crop
of golden hair. We were inseparable
companions, and there is not an experience
of my child life with which her memory is
not allied. The first definite recollection I
have of her, is that of a May day long ago,
when I lost myself in the deep woods while
gathering flowers, and sat me down in her
company to wait for God to come to our
relief. So implicit was that little child's
faith that He would come, that I felt no fear
when the shadows fell around me, and into
the depths of the twilight sky, one by one
stole the silvery stars.

I remember just how the thrushes sang in the tops of the tall trees, and how long it seemed before our deliverance came. I remember questioning her, as we sat on our bed of moss, how she thought it possible that God could have been started without anybody to make Him, and if she really believed He was going to go on living for-ever, and forever, and forever! The thought grew too heavy at last for our little minds to uplift, and we lay back on our velvet couch, and looked away into the depths of the starry sky and wept for very wonder.

I remember how we cheered one another by enacting the drama of the deserted babes, and gently wooed the twilight birds to cover us with leaves, a proceeding which they de-clined to carry out with many twitters of sleepy song.

I date the memory of my little friend chiefly from this experience, for the reason that then, for the first time, we were left alone, and dependent upon one another for comfort and cheer. After that afternoon she and I were often by ourselves. We found a nest away up among the singing branches of a willow tree where we used to

lie for hours, and dream our fairy dreams
together. There we often sought to solve
the riddle of a strange perplexing world.
What was the power which curved the great
blue sky above our heads, and kept the
sun and stars in place upon it? Whence
came the winds, and whither did they go?
Why, without note of warning or sound of
rushing wings, did great clouds rush into
the sky, and what voice was that which
spoke in thunder from the shadowed hills?
What was the lightning, and who kindled
it? Why did the wild rose always bear
the same kind of flower, and the apple tree
never forget itself and put forth a plum?
What made the bee blunder so awkwardly
against the holly hocks, and settle within
their flaring cups with such an endless fret
and flurry? Who taught the birds to build
their nests? and was all the music of the
earth copied from the score of their minstrel
notes? Why did the blue-dragon fly never
sit still, and was it kind in God to let the
"devil's darning needle" sew up little children's ears? Where would we go when we
died, as Neighbor Jordan's baby did, and
was it not wicked to leave a baby all alone
in the grave-yard with nobody nigh to

keep it warm and cuddled? What was a ghost, and did it really walk about at mid-night in a white sheet? Wouldn't we be apt to get tired singing psalm-tunes up in heaven forever? And wouldn't it be nice if God would keep a special place for little girls who didn't care to sing or play on harps? If a bird could fly in the air, why couldn't a little girl with a big umbrella? If heaven was just the other side of the sky, why didn't the angels ever fall through? Perhaps the stars were their shining feet twinkling over the crystal floor! Who made the grass know just when to turn green, or told the trees when to unfold their leaves?

These are but a few of the questions that we were wont to ponder, and, although the years are many since we rocked together in our willow-bough cradle, the answer has never yet been revealed. She, perhaps, has learned the mystery of it all, for she left me suddenly one day never to return, and perhaps in the mystic land whither she has vanished, the secrets of nature are all revealed.

She was a truthful creature, that blessed little girl, and her heart was pure as unstained snow. She was trustful, and confiding, and tender, too. She thought no evil, and she did no wrong. Beyond a childish naughtiness now and then, her baby soul was free from the defilement of sin.

Ah, me, the difference between us now! I hold in my hands, to-night, the withered stalk whereon life's rose should blossom fair and dewy-sweet, and find it bears but a few scorched and wind-torn leaves! Could but my childhood's angel have tarried with me, would not these flowers have kept their freshness and their fragrance to the last?

None but God can tell why she left me, and why, deprived of her presence, I have grown so far away from heaven. Can it be that she went because I grew to ridicule her pretty faiths and simple creeds? We first fell out over "Santa Claus" and came to open rupture I remember, when I laughed at her idea that he lived in a palace in the Northern Lights, and kept a herd of immortal reindeers. We grew farther and farther apart each year, in our belief that new-born mortals were found in the trunks of hollow trees, and that the angels laid them there fresh from the arms of God. Her assertion that every time a baby smiled in its sleep, the cherub angels

10

were whispering in its little pink ear, made
me laugh, and gradually created a coldness
between us.

For a long time she continued to accom-
pany me wherever I went, and with whom-
ever I chose to walk, but when the village
boys began by and by to try and turn our
heads with flattery, and gently chaffed her
simple ways, she drew aside and only
watched me from afar. But though sun-
dered by day, we never slept apart, and it
was she who for long years kept up the simple habit of repeating the prayer we learned
together at our mother's knee.

The day she left me, to return no more,
I never can forget! She carried with her
so much that made life radiant, that looking backward to-night, a long way on my
journey towards the beautiful gate, I shade
my dazzled eyes, as one watching from a
shadowy land the break of golden billows
beneath a sparkling sun. We had been
growing farther and farther apart for a
long time, until it came to be that only ,
at prayer time, or during the singing of
some heavenly hymn, or when picking
flowers together on a fair spring morning,
when God seemed very near to us, we held

counsel. She had grown so etherial of presence that she seemed scarcely more than a spirit standing by my side, as impalpable as a wreath of mist, or a falling flake of downy snow. I stood before my mirror, one day, dressed for my coming out party. About my neck were clasped the first jewels I had ever worn and in my heart the happy consciousness that I was free to enter the untried realm of womanhood, and gather its roses (I knew nothing then of its thorns!) thrilled my soul with foolish joy! Just behind me, her dim eyes full of tears, her lips tremulous with a smile of unutterable longing and love, I saw my Child Angel, my little constant friend and companion. From those sweet lips there came, like the chime of unseen and far-off silver bells, these words:

"Farewell! You have no further need of me! My ways are no longer your ways, nor my thoughts your thoughts. You have put aside the things that made us one; you are entering upon a life where I cannot follow. Farewell! a long, but not an eternal farewell. For, when tired out and disappointed, your hands torn and bleeding with the thorns you must gather with your roses,

your heart emptied of its dreams, and sigh-
ing, for the innocent delights of those days
which we have spent together, your feet
draw near the gate which naught but your
dying breath can waft ajar, I will meet you
again, and lead you very gently along the
way that shall bring you at last to the presence of your God, and into everlasting
peace and rest."

Thus saying, my child-nature departed.
The angel in me stole heavenward again,
and left me what I am.

"Six months pass sometimes between
the glimpses I get of friend or neighbor
outside of my own household."

The above sentence in a letter just received from a woman who has lived for the
past ten years on a ranch away out West
has set me thinking very tenderly to-night
of lonely women.

There is always some variety in a man's
life which lifts it out of monotony. The
wood-chopper, whose strong, vehement
strokes lay the forest monarch low, its

leafy crown never again to uplift itself joy-
ously in the sun-bright spaces of the air,
works hard and goes home tired, but the
labor he has accomplished hasn't dulled his
faculties nor benumbed his very life currents, as the unending drudgery of his
duties have affected the wife who has stayed
within doors all day long, washing dishes,
peeling potatoes, baking bread, patching
trousers and nursing babies. For her there
is no stepping off the treadmill, no change
of scene, until the last hour which drops the
tattered old curtain, extinguishes the glim-
mering lights and proclaims the long and
stupid drama ended. It seems a very pretentious thing to attempt a word of cheer
and solace for such lives. God knows they
need it, though—a hand stretched out, a
song dropped in the night, to revive long-
slumbering hope. When I see, as I sometimes do, a sensitive, delicate nature with
a heart like May sunshine, shedding its
brightness in a home and upon hearts as
unappreciative as is a glacier of the sun-
bright rays that dance and quiver above its
frozen bosom; when I see such a soul, created to shine and cheer and bless, struggling for existence, and mated to a life as

cold and bloodless as a shoal of shad, I am
tempted to wonder if eternal vigilance is not
at fault, fallen asleep like the watch on deck
and letting human lives go to pieces on the
breakers that might have outridden all the
billows of the sea and entered triumphant
into the port of peace. Everything seems
haphazard as to the adjustment of destinies
half the time. The woman fitted to adorn
any sphere gets shunted off on a side track,
and is unnoticed and forgotten, while some
empty-headed sister whom it would have
been a special mercy to have obliterated
flashes down the main track in all the glory
of screaming whistle and flying flag.

My dear, the only way to conquer a cast-
iron destiny is to yield to it.   You will
break to pieces if you are always casting
yourself against a rock. Sit down on the
"sorrowing stone" now and then; you cannot help it, but don't go on flinging yourself headlong against it. If life holds nothing finer and sweeter than the routine of
uncongenial labor, if all the pleasant dreams
and hopes of youth remain but as fabrics
from which the bright colors are washed
away, if ambition and joy and spirit were
drowned long ago in that unstayed flood

of dishwater which has proved the watery grave of many a brilliant career, if goodly intention and noble purpose glimmered only a little now and then from out the murky environments of your life like fisher lights at sea, accept the inevitable bravely, like a soldier undergoing hardships but sure of something better to come. Do not sit down and cry over those poor old "might have beens" like children shedding tears over last year's broken dandelion chains. Just accept your hard lot as students do allotted tasks, content to know that by and bye will surely bring vacation time, the unending holidays and home. Remember how many otherwise sweet natures lie all about us, spoiled by prosperity like over ripe apples in the sun. Perhaps had Providence granted you the fulfillment of all your hopes you would have become joined to your idols, with no higher aspirations than worldly things. If your lot is cast desolate and alone, and yet if heaven has given you children, mold the lives of those children into heroes and gentlewomen as brave and sweet as ever brightened the courts of kings. What need have you to repine at your loneliness when God has made of every mother a divine sculptor, to create gods and goddesses in her own workshop. In the guidance and training of those precious souls you have work enough to do to forbid an idle or a repining moment. Above all, cultivate the small opportunities you have. Learn patience through the repeated overthrow of patience, sweetness through trial, and strength through defeat, remembering that we do not grow so much by externals as we do by the impulses within us that set our thoughts heavenward. We cannot be thwarted by any evil that does not find lodgment in our hearts any more than a lily can be changed into a wild parsnip by a lot of little boys pegging putty-balls at it. Nothing can stop us if we are bound to grow. He alone is our judge, to Him alone shall we yield the record of life's troubled day, and I think His very first word, His first smile, will waft away the memory of our loneliness and our tears as dust is wafted before the summer wind.

There is just one thing in the latter part of the nineteenth century that never fails to bring success, and that is assurance. If you are going to make yourself known it is no longer the thing to quietly pass out a visiting card—you must advance with a trumpet and blow a brazen blast to shake the stars. The time has gone by when self-advancement can be gained by modest and unassuming methods. To stand with a lifted hat and solicit a hearing savors of mendicancy and an humble spirit. The easily abashed and the diffident may starve in a garret, or go die on the highways— there is no chance for them in the jostling rush of life. The gilded circus chariot, with a full brass band and a plump goddess distributing circulars, is what takes the popular heart by storm. Your silent entry into town, depending upon the merits of your wares to gain an audience or work up a custom, is chimerical and obsolete. We no longer sit in the shadow and play flutes; we mount a pine platform and blow on a trombone, and in that way we draw a crowd, and that is what we live for. Who are the women who succeed in business ventures of any sort? Mostly the mannish, bold, aggressive amazons who are unmindful of rebuffs and impervious to contempt. Who are the men who wear diamonds and live easy lives? Largely the politicians who have made their reputation in bar-room rostrums and among sharpers. Oh, for a wind to blow us forward a hundred years out of this age of sordid self-seeking and impudent assertiveness into something larger and sweeter and finer. Give us less yeast in our bread and more substance; fill our cups with wine rather than froth, and for sweet pity's sake hang up the great American trumpet and let "silence, like a poultice, come to heal the blows of sound."

I had entertained some thought of investing in Blank's Sarsaparilla as a family blood purifier, but since my tour Eastward I have decided to perish, with every member of my family, of eczema and go to my grave tattooed with boils rather than encourage the shameless proprietors of that much-advertised drug. There is not a moss-covered roof, nor a rocky bluff, nor a modest fence-post between here and the Atlantic coast that is not lettered in flaring yellow char-

acters a foot long: "Take Blank's Sarsaparilla." Along the beautiful Mohawk
Valley, where bonnie Eloise once flitted like
a fairy, the stern mandate confronts you:
"Take Blank's Sarsaparilla." Where Niagara flings out its emerald colors to leap
the rainbow-tinted chasm, just over the way
from the railroad track gleams the hideous
behest: "Take Blank's Sarsaparilla."
Every village is skirted with it, and in Utica
I believe it was that I saw an aged darky
whose back was emblazoned with the text.
One of the things that will have to be elim-
inated from the future, to make it heaven,
will be the sordid greed of human nature.
Next to the man who wantonly cuts down
a tree, or shoots meadow larks for pie, or
turns his front yard into a potato patch, is
the man who rents out his barn roof or the
big rock in his pasture land for advertising
drugs.

Well, I have seen a ballet at last worth
seeing. It was the other night at the Madi-
son Square Garden in New York. Somebody came home late with tickets, and proposed we go over and hear the wonderful

Strauss and see the ballet of which the papers had so much to say. Then what a scurrying there was for bonnets and things. How strange it is that a woman is so constructed that she can never take a sudden start. If necessity calls a man to Europe all he has to do is to fling his things into a grip along with a box of cigars, put on his hat and go. But a woman has to shop and fume and fret until she would be too tired to enjoy paradise if she ever got there. But in spite of being a quarter of an hour late, the concert had not commenced when we took our seats. The building is the Auditorium in willow and water colors. There is space without massiveness and sumptuousness. The seating capacity is, if I remember rightly, about seventy thousand. Perhaps I may be mistaken, but according to my recollection the above figures were mentioned to me as correct. The background of the great stage represented chaos. Creation had not yet been evolved when the artist took his stand to paint that background. An infinitude of clouds, somber and tipped with gold, fleecy as young lamb's wool, yet bearing terrible suggestions of thunderbolts and tornadoes in their

disordered bosom. Presently out stepped
a dapper little fellow, raised his baton and
the music commenced. If that was Strauss,
at first I was disappointed. But as I
watched him the wonder grew that one
small man could so embody music's self.
Every movement was a harmony. The wave
of his baton brought music in showers from
the very air. Crescendos and diminuendos
rained about him like water drops. His
face, so calm and yet so strong, shone like
a flame above the orchestra that followed
every move of his baton as a magnet the
steel. The tempo of the Strauss music is
almost too fast for dancing. Butterflies
in the sunshine, or sparks in a high wind, or
leaves in a gale, might keep step to the
waltzes, but slow-footed mortals must fall
far behind. After the music came the ballet. The scene was laid among the flowers,
in the dawn of a June morning. Columbia
was about to choose her favorite. Tall
branches of white lilies waved sleepily, violets slept at the foot of mossy banks, roses
bloomed against green trellises, fuchsias
and daisies, daffodils and dandelions, snow-
drops and tulips, every flower possible to
name, was grouped about the stage.

Suddenly one of the clouds opened and a sylph in silver gray, poised by invisible wires, floated above the garden. She represented the South wind, whose mission it was to awaken the flowers. Gradually the insects awoke and joined together in a wavering dance. Butterflies, dragonflies, katydids and bumble-bees, all superbly costumed, darted in and out between the groups of garden beauties. The day grew and the clouds were tinted with sunrise tints. Then the flowers awoke and were drawn into the mazes of the dance. At this point the vast stage displayed a wealth of color impossible to describe. Imagine a garden full of all the varieties of flowers known to tropic lands in motion. The music was grand, and the dancing something to dream about. Columbia in seeking her favorite flower summoned each one before her throne. None charmed her as the golden-rod, bedecked in plumes of dusty yellow and wound about with sheaves of green. At last, throned on a pedestal and royal in vivid calcium lights, this flower was crowned the queen of floral realm and favorite of Columbia's flowers. The scenic splendors were hidden away behind green curtains, and the evening's entertainment was at an end. Seated near us during the hours of our tarrying in the hall was a group that I mourn to think I shall never meet again. A father and his two daughters, who seemed each one to have stepped from out the covers of a romance. Where do you find in actual life such courtly manners and such girlish grace? No furbelows, no bangs, no frills. The dignity of the gentleman and a certain humorous twinkle in his clear eye, combined with the unconscious manners of the daughters, their enthusiasm and their fresh young beauty, convinced me that they were visions and not actualities in this hoidenish and self-seeking age. A supper at Delmonico's to round off the music and the ballet proved the capstone to an edifice that might have been built in Spain. Chicago has no Delmonico's; there is but one on earth, and New York claims it.

Do you never feel like calling out to the galloping years to come to a halt? This break-neck race of time is going to land us all too soon over the border. For my part I would like to slow up for awhile. I see my neighbor growing gray; I wonder how my own head looks. I see the children of yesterday wheeling perambulators for their own little "bald-headed tyrants," and it strikes me that at this rate you and I will be old folks before we know it. The Christmases come and go like the wooden animals on a carousal ring; while the band plays and the children laugh a dozen revolutions are finished. It used to be a good long time from Christmas to Christmas, but now it is like the dip of a swallow's wing or the shadow of a cloud. I think the calendars are not so reliable as they used to be. The seasons are constant, but they are in a greater hurry. Spring used to take off her things and sit awhile; now she only stops to throw a bunch of lilacs in at the window and flits away. Summer and autumn used to make themselves at home and linger long and pleasantly, but of late years the former weaves a garland which is hardly finished before the latter breathes upon it and it drops to pieces. As for winter, he barely

takes time to show us his wares of diamonds and ermine and laces before he is
summoned back to the land of nowhere.
God bless us, every one.   Where shall we
all be this time fifty twelve-months?

CHAPTER IV.

"I stood on the bridge at midnight."

Over my head the silent heaven, flecked
with the fine dust of stars; at my feet the
dark river, with a score of changeful lights
that flash like jewels upon the dusky tide.
As far as the eye can reach on either hand
the lights of a great city, whose confines
cannot be reckoned in the gloom, and whose
wide sweep an eagle's wing would tire to
traverse.   Over the river, betwixt its murky
waves and the far-off stars, a bridge, worn
with the tread of constant feet.   Upon this
rickety highway has fallen the hush of the
night hours, and only an occasional foot-fall
tramps by the spot where I loiter.   In my
face there blows a fresh, sweet breath from
the lake, far out upon the unseen billows of
which a thousand sails are beating land-
ward.   The big world, in which a few insignificant atoms called "you" and "I," respect-
ively, strut so pompously to and fro, is hush-

ing away to its brief night's respite from toil. And when "you" and "I" have been dead so many years, my dear, that our dust shall have passed into forests, that in their turn shall have withered and died, this ebb and flow of humanity's sullen tide shall still beat on. The little game we call life, and mourn to lose, shall have been long over for generations yet to come, while these nights and days of troubled existence course on like untired chargers to a distant goal.

Oh, host without number, who live and laugh, and weep and die all about me, I stand for a moment here between the river and the stars, and am filled with wonder at the mystery of your being. What endless volumes of life's experience are being laid over leaf by leaf to-night under the great city's myriad of lamps. There are lights amid your many that are lighted in the homes of the prosperous and the happy; there are waning candles that aid the tardy seamstress in her ill-requited toil; there are tapers that fitfully burn at the feet of the dead; there are lights that flash in the gilded halls of sin; there is the pale student's paler candle, and the miser's, as he greedily counts his gold. The young mother bends

with one above the bed of her ailing first-
born; the neglected wife weeps by one
whose flickering beam but reveals the desolation of her home; the business man lingers by one to settle the balance for the
day; the gambler gathers together his ill-
gotten gains by one, and before another the
drunkard unsteadily lifts his glass to mark
the ruddy glow of the poison that has murdered his manhood.

There are ten thousand breaking hearts
over there amid the shadow; there are ten
thousand breasts in which joy is unfolding
like a rose; there are ten thousand souls bat-
tling with temptation, and, ah, me! there
are ten thousand yielding to the syren voice,
while still another ten thousand are coming
out more than conquerers in the strife.
There are souls jostling one another in the
mystic corridors of life, ten thousand going
out into death's forgetfulness, ten thousand
coming into the heritage of life.

Not the mystery of the stars above us is
so great as is the mystery of life that sur-
rounds us. They circle in an orbit pre-des-
tined for them from time's beginning. Not
so with a soul, struck like a spark from infinitude, and soon bewildered with the mys-

tery we call living. What wonder we go astray? What wonder we are lost? What wonder we fall? Standing here in the midnight and looking about me at the far gleaming lights, each one of which marks some event of individual life—filled with the grandeur of the scene, yet also filled with sorrow and shame for the revelations those lights disclose to all-seeing heaven, the old terror of the inevitable sweeps over me again, as it used, when a bit of a girl, I covered my head in the bed clothes to think, that, try as I would, I could never, never, never, get away from God! The sense of individual powerlessness overcomes me. The hopelessness of any belief that He who sits above and watches the unequal struggle, should care for the destiny of such blind moles as we, so overpowers my faith that I fain would dash over the side of the rickety old bridge and find in death the welcome peace of everlasting oblivion.

I want to tell you, before I go, of something I saw take place on State street the other day. A dirty-faced, ragged little urchin was poking about in the ash-barrels for spoils. He had a mite of a dog with him, quite as unkempt and uncared for as himself. But around that dog's neck, if you please, was tied a bow of faded red ribbon, and his incessant gambols and pranks found favor in the sight of his beggar-boy master, filling his heart with pride and satisfaction. If you can call so uncouth and unreasonable an instinct by the sacred name of love, then indeed it was plain to see that the boy loved the dog, and between the two there was the complete understanding of mutual affection. Suddenly, while the dog was bounding and barking in the exuberance of canine joy, and his master's eyes were sparkling with relish of this one thing in life that was his very own—as much to him as your greatest treasure is to you—there came a rapidly-driven dray down the crowded street. A moment later I saw a ragged boy, with set face and anguished eye, gather in his arms a maimed and dying dog, and gently walk away. What had happened? Only a worthless street cur trampled to death. Only a miserable little rag-picker robbed of the sole bit of joy and comfort his life ever knew—the one friend that loved him—that was all. But there was a look in the boy's face that will keep my heart aching for many a day to come, and the fluttering bit of fancy ribbon about the dead dog's neck brought a mist to my eyes that hid the splendor of the morning.

Some day, perhaps, I shall ride in a Chicago hansom cab. But it will be when I am dead. No living power, no sudden emergency, could put me inside one of those adult perambulators again. The man who drives thinks more of a quarter than of any chance to prolong his miserable fare's life. His sole and only aim seems to be to hurl you through to your destination and return for another victim. I rode in a hansom once, and since then I have been unmistakably grayheaded. In the first place, the horse developed acute delirium the moment I was shut behind the cab's breast-plate, and pranced down the street on three legs, snorting like a war steed. This would have been quite enough without

a wheel coming off. But there are some
people born to drain every cup to the dregs.
All that was conceivable of mental anguish
and special torment I experienced on that
ride, and when a policeman picked me up
from the cable track, where I was finally
spilled in the path of an advancing grip, I
registered a vow thenceforth to abjure han-
soms.

Once there was a mouse which lived in
such constant dread of being devoured by
a cat that a magician who dwelt near by
and whose rest was disturbed by reason of
the lamentations of the mouse, changed it
into a cat, saying: "There, have done with
your whimpering, be a cat and fear no
more." No sooner did the mouse become
a cat, however, than its dread of being wor-
ried by a dog gave it no rest. "Here, then,"
said the good-natured magician, "be a dog
and end your fears." But, alack and alas,
when the cat became a dog its fears were
tenfold greater than ever before, lest a tiger
should drink its blood.   So the obliging
wizard turned it into a tiger, and cried,

"Now have done with fear, you can defy
all!" But the tiger slunk into the jun-
gle, and was afraid to come forth for dread
that a huntsman's rifle should lay him low.
Then the thoroughly disgusted wizard
turned the coward back into the primal
mouse, saying, "You have but the heart of
a mouse—be a mouse!"

Every day I meet with people beneath
the tiger-skin from whose outward seeming
peep forth the beady eyes of the mouse.
People who have all they can ask for—a
competency, good health, an unbroken
household band, and a faithful heart to in-
terpose between them and the world's ar-
rows—and yet are always dreading troubles
that will probably never overtake them, and
consume their vitality and wither their freshness by worrying over the inevitable cares
and the little annoyances that are as inseparable from life as is the bark from the tree
or the brier from the rose. They are forever deploring the shadowy side of life, as
though shadows were anything more than
the proof of the shining of the sun. They
have presentiments, and are versed in the
lore of dreams. If they have children, instead of enjoying the God-given treasures,

they are always dreading diseases that shall waste and destroy, or accidents that shall cripple or kill. Scarlet fever stands over against every air-castle they build for their darling's future, and plants its blood-red banner on the highest turret. They are like out-riders, plunging at full gallop in the desire to cross bridges without waiting for the steady march of the hours to bring us all to tread their planks.

How many Christian women there are whose black ingratitude to God would shame the ingrate heart of earth's most noted traitors. They forget present blessings in worrying about a future they have nothing to do with. They are like children who sit at a bountiful table, and instead of eating spend their time in crying lest they should have no dinner to-morrow.

Now, what is going to help these mouse-hearted people? Religion? No; not in its orthodox formula. Bible texts and faith-circulars or set prayers? I think not, without common sense and a grain of philosophy. Prayer to God without using common sense is an impertinence. God is never going to stop the heavenly councils to help you buy winter flannels, or decide whether

you shall go down town or remain at home.
A healthy child who hangs upon its father
and does not take a single step without
asking guidance is either an idiot or a nui-
sance. Having learned to walk, let him use
his feet. If you have common sense make
use of it, and don't expect a special miracle
to be wrought in your behalf when a little
reason and a proper use of the faculties God
gave you will carry you through.

The law of all living is rigid. Either we
are masters or we are mastered. If we are
masters, we are like soldiers drilled to know
no fear; we go forth to meet destiny with
the steady eye and the unflinching front of
disciplined forces. If we are mastered we
meet destiny as a mob scatters at the first
rifle shot. Whatever be in store for me,
from a toothache to a cyclone, if I make up
my mind to master the dread of it, as far as
possible, to wait until it comes before I
quail, and then to meet it like a Roman
rather than like a hound, no matter what
the sequence may be, "even unto death," I
shall have conquered.

Build for the future, learn from the past,
but live in the present. Did you ever stop
to think, you mouse-hearts, the harmony of

whose lives are all turned into discord by forecasting trouble, to whom a few flies in the dining room or pencil marks on the paint, or the tracing of little fingers on the crystal clearness of the window-pane brings a load of care and the indulgence of a shrewish tongue; did you ever stop to think, I say, what you will do when some of the really great troubles of life shall sweep down upon you like a wind out of a northern sky? Will you remember these magpie vexations when the feet that made the muddy tracks that shattered your dainty place shall have turned aside, have climbed the heavenward slopes, and walk with God? When the hands that traced the finger-marks shall have loosened their caressing clasp from yours, and leave you only dreams of the rose-leaf touch that once thrilled the mother-heart within you. Ah, I think, my dear, when those troubles do come upon you, you will not take note of flies in the dining room, nor stop to scold over a disordered room.

There is 'nothing like absence to sweeten association. I have always held that it is

living too constantly in one another's so-
city that cools love between husbands and
wives. Occasional separation would preserve first impressions. Take any good
thing and make a steady diet of it and the
appetite fails. Even strawberries would
pall if every month in the year yielded them.
It is only because it tarries briefly within
the circuit of the twelve months that the
rosy fruit is inimitable. For that reason
I expect when I get home from this Tophet-
like trip of mine to swear a new allegiance
to my friends and cancel the dislike I bear
my enemies.

One night not so very long ago our
household was awakened simultaneously
by a noise like the bursting of a ripe cyclone.
The dreadful sound fell into the midst of the
night's heaviest sleep, and created a panic.
I bounded out of bed, and with the young
person hanging on to one arm and the boy
loudly lamenting from his couch in the
corner, began a search for matches. The
darkness was dense; one could have carved
it like old cheese. There was an ominous

silence in the gloom, as though nature was rallying itself for another shock. I groped my way to the bureau and fingered every inch of its crowded top in vain. There were pin-balls and bottles of perfume, hair-pins, hat-pins, glove-boxes, toilet water and pow-der-puffs, but no matches. I prowled away in another direction, and tackled the wash-stand; tipped over the tooth-brush holder, drenched my toes with the contents of the toilet pitcher, dabbled my fingers in cold cream, toyed with the soap, but as the Irish-man tellingly puts it, "the divil" a match I found. Then I struck the side of the bed and fell over into space with a racket that renewed the lamentation of the invisible boy, and caused the faithful young person to release her hold and wander away into darkness on her own account. But finally, glory be to praise! my fingers encountered the slender little pine fragment for which I pined. "I have got one!" I shouted in glee, and at the cry the noise of the weeping ceased, and hope sprang to life in every breast. Eagerly I drew the match along the under surface of the shelf; it gave forth no spark! Again, and yet again I tried it, until disgusted I threw it far from me into the night and reviled the hideous mockery of a burnt match in time of need. Far better to have found nothing than set one's hopes of deliverance on such a useless thing. The darkness was tenfold harder to bear after the cruel disappointment, and even the gaining of a light in course of time could not dispel the unheroic rage that had accompanied the first defeat.

Are there not, among other types, lots of people in the world who serve the same irritating and exasperating purposes that burnt matches do in the hour of man's extremity? We set our hopes upon them; we pin our faith to them; we rely upon, idealize, glorify them, but when circumstances put them to the test, though we draw them ever so smartly along the crisis of the hour, they emit no responsive spark. They are all wood and no tinder. A damp tooth-pick would answer quite as well to bring about the illumination of either understanding or soul of which we stand in need.

Half the marriages of the present day turn out in the hour of test as my burnt match did. It is all very well while life needs no illumination, while the sun shines, and the matches and the candles are kept in their fancy little nickel boxes and their artistic scones upon the shelf. But when the night hangs heavy in the sky and out of the fancied dream of peace like a thunderbolt falls the shock of sudden alarm, how then? Love strikes the match, and behold it is burnt at both ends. Worthless in the hour of need, and so love wanders away in the deepening shadows never to return. Look to it when you marry that your stock of light producers is kept in a dry and convenient place, ready for instant service. And see to it that your protestations are tipped with the reliable article, and not already burnt and consumed in the fires of an unworthy past.

The parents who fail their children in the crisis of their needs; the mother who is off to a party or to the theater while her little ones learn to forget her in the company of hired nurses or unworthy companionship; the father who becomes an utter stranger to his growing family in order that he may make money or court political preference; the mother who thinks more of fashion and of social success than of the delicate longings and aspirations of her maiden daugh-

ter's heart; the father who is never on hand
to mingle in the children's joys and griefs;
the mother who neglects her duty and casts
obloquy upon the sacred name of mother,
are nothing better in God's sight than
burnt matches in the world's workshop.
Away with such superfluities! Their room
is better than their permitted cumbering of
time. I say it in all solemnity, but for my
part I would rather die right now while
there is a little of the illuminating power
left in heart and brain, even if the crucial
test sometimes charges the air with the
evanescent fumes of sulphur, than live to
be a burnt out match, kept in a box along
with other used-up forces; of no good to
either God or man, and only capable now
and then of raising a whirlwind of rage in
some human creature's breast, who, mistak-
ing me for what I never more can be, has
set his hopes of present or eternal welfare
and deliverance upon the illumination it is
no longer in my power to give. Amen!

I love to spend money. Indeed, it has a
way of burning itself through my pocket

12

like a sun-glass through tissue; but I do
like to gain my money's equivalent. Take
a trip in a stuffy sleeper, with the ther-
mometer at 98 and a black duke of a porter
to look down upon you, let the windows
all day look out upon the sand dunes of the
desert; let the flies infest the air with their
awful presence, and allow dust to sift into
every one of the million pores of your tortured body, and if you call that an equivalent for a hard-earned handful of dollars
you would call a morning's engagement
with a dentist a holiday and cramps a picnic.

Some day I am going to build me a
home. It may not be here; I may have
gone "over the hills" and found the happy
valley before I start to dig its foundation;
but I shall surely build it. It shall stand
upon a bluff and overlook the sea; there
shall be a grove of silver birches under its
windows, and all day long the soft wind,
like a bee, shall drone and hum within its
flickering shadows. The road that leads to
it shall wind through woodland ways, and

nobody who comes on any but a friendly errand shall find a clue to the labyrinth. An Æolian harp shall be strung within the northward facing window, so that when the storms sweep down upon that part of the world where stands my happy home they shall advance to the beat of music. In the garden shall grow the sweet, old-fashioned flowers of long ago; the hollyhock with its silken leaves and its pollen finer than the dust of gold shall fringe the sunny borders; the larkspur and the four-o'clock shall run riot in the untrimmed garden beds; marigold, like dusky stars, shall light the way for troops of curtesying columbine and fragrant pinks to follow. Annunciation lilies shall be ever at their prayers like vestal nuns in dim cloisters of that lovely garden, and the rose shall preempt her claim to every nook within its magic circle. There the tawny tiger lily and the splendid nasturtium shall hold their court, and the pansy from a thousand coverts shall lift its bright face to greet the day. "Bachelor's buttons" and "widow's tears" and "bleeding hearts" shall find a place, while "Sweet Williams" and "Bouncing Bettys" shall never be turned away. There shall be so

many flowers blooming, and so many butterflies glancing, and so many birds singing
in that garden of delight that the perfume
and the melody shall make all the country
side for miles and miles about a veritable
land of enchantment for those who journey
by. There shall be no such thing as a
lawn-mower known within the precincts of
my garden; there shall be no clipped shrubs,
no trimmed walks, no stiff beds. No fountain shall be forced to play therein, and no
statue or device of any kind to suggest the
world of art shall desecrate nature's domain. The steps that lead up to my home
shall be low and broad and the entrance
door shall be of unpolished cedar, with a
massive brass knocker to herald the approach of welcome guests. There shall be
but one room on the ground floor, and that
shall be of feudal dimension and cheer.
Beautiful screens of quaint design shall
serve to partition off this great room as my
fancy may desire, but at will they shall all
be laid aside and the room become a royal
hospitality hall. Four immense fireplaces
shall glorify it, and the light shall enter from
every side, and also from the roof, which
shall be so adjusted as to allow the air of

heaven to enter at will. There shall be no paint or varnish about my house—natural woods, well oiled to preserve and enhance the native grain, shall be its only decoration. The kitchen shall be completely detached from the main building. The sleeping rooms shall open from an upper corridor reached by a winding stairway. The bath-room shall be of Pompeiian marble, made to represent cool grottoes under the sea. There shall be no modern improvements such as drains or sewer connections, fur-naces nor electric bells and lights under-neath its roof. Inscriptions of the choicest shall be engraved upon the walls and mosaiced within the floors. Over the bed-room doors shall be painted sprays of lan-guid poppies and purple heartsease for pleasant thoughts. There shall be no two articles of furniture alike in all the house, no horrible suits, no stuffy upholstery, no dusty carpets. The rugs shall be of tapestry and all the hangings of wrought silk. Music shall be the spirit of the home, and sun-shine, sweet air and hygiene its handmaids. Within it every tired woman and over-worked child and discouraged bread-winner in the land shall find a welcome, and there shall be no such thing as an alarm clock or a rising bell or the distant whistle of an approaching train, heard forever. If you come to visit me, my tired friend, you shall instantly be presented with a velvet dressing gown and a pair of swan-down slippers, and you shall have leave to lie down on a lounge constructed of feathers and springs, where you may read novels and eat chocolate bon-bons for months at a time. You and I shall fathom at last the meaning of the word "rest," so long unknown in our vocabulary. We shall be as lazy as the lizard that basks in the shade of a Mexican cactus, as sleepy as a white owl, and as free from care as a lotus flower on the Nile. I cannot exactly say when the invitations will be out for this reunion of rest, this carnival of the lazy, but be assured, my dear, you shall be one of the remembered ones when I come into the heritage of my dreams.

N. B.—I omitted to mention that no "canned goods" will be served in my ideal home.

That household can never be called mo-notonous that boasts the possession of nine

cats. Exactly that number of gentle felines
sit about my humble threshold and make
the home rhythmical with cry of battle and
vice versa. Each one is a fighter from
"away back." There is Robert Elsmere,
who from his name might be expected to
suffer the pangs of a perturbed spirit. He
bears the scars of many onslaughts, yet allows no opportunity to escape him to get
in a left-hander at his world in general. If
he can hurl defiance at nothing else he has
been known to attack the cow and spit and
storm at that peaceful bovine like a bee
storming a buttress. There is the "African
Farm," a coal-black creature with eyes like
emeralds set in jet. She spends most of her
time shrieking for milk, which she will accept only well warmed and unskimmed.
There is Swipes, after whom the whole family chase from morn to night, seeking to
deter him from his proclivity for killing
robins. I have vowed a vow that the very
next red-breast Swipes destroys I buy a
dime's worth of chloroform and away goes
his depraved spirit to the land of the here-
after. There is Imbecile, who as his
name would indicate is hardly responsible
for his ravages upon the family larder. He

does nothing but eat and blink. The day will shortly come when I shall throw a stove-lid at him and abruptly close his career. There is Jenness Miller, so called from an appearance about the legs as though swathed in a divided skirt; and Thomas Z. Pratt, named at random and filling his place as patriarch of the flock with a dignity a city father might emulate. I am a hard-working woman, put to my wit's end often as to how to make both ends of a slender income meet, and for that reason I am filled with joy as my family of dependent cats increase upon my hands. I am too much of a humanitarian, both in theory and in practice, to allow the goblin brood to starve, and yet to feed them properly so that they will not forage among the robins taxes the resources of a dauntless spirit. I can get nobody to kill them. I have not the nerve myself to do so, consequently I see before me an ever-darkening future. Won't somebody advise me what to do? More cats mean a pauper's grave for Amber.

There was a young woman of Norway,
Who casually sat in her doorway,
  When the door jammed her flat
  She cried, "What of that?"
This indifferent young woman of Norway.

Alas, for a tithe of thy philosophy, O brave Norwegian damsel! Would that the sublime supremacy of mind over matter that has placed thee on record as the first of mental scientists might visit a few of us! What to thee the horror of accumulated sewing, of an empty purse and an emptier coal bin! What to thee the revilings of thy Norwegian lord when bread chanced to be sour and coffee aqueous? What to thee the incoming and outgoing caravan of kitchen help? When the infant Norwegians tear their knickerbockers, or the wee one of all swallows copper cents, or broken glass, or any other deadly compound; when the chimney smokes, or the roof leaks, or the chariot of the unannounced guest draws up to thy gates, with not even a ham bone in the larder for cheer, never does thy sublime unconcern forsake thee, thou daughter of a frost-blooded tribe. I salute thee, across the sea, and across the year, and drink a beaker of beer to the perpetuation of thy indifference in a progeny that shall never perish!

I wonder if there is one of all who read and feel an interest in these columns who can rise up and say, "Lo! I am one whom the small annoyances of life never fret."

Is there one of the number who has never seen the time when the little foxes have not bitten the bloom away from the vines and left them bare? It is very well to summon a certain amount of philosophy to the rescue, and say that a life is unacquainted with true sorrow that knows nothing harsher than the worriment of domestic care, but I tell you right now, there's many a woman has gone down to her death with a prospect of a martyr's crown from the endurance of just these things! Not all the martyrs have perished amid blazing fagots!

The big trials of life generally find us prepared, and a special strength is vouchsafed us to meet them, but for the souls that are beset behind and before with the torments of daily recurring care, who shall tell the number of their discouragements?

Put me in a three-acre lot and bid me run for my life to escape from a roaring bull, and the chances are that your humble servant will place a five-barred fence between her and the horns of her pursuer in pretty quick time, but bid me run from a swarm of hornets and I fall discouraged by the way.

There is something heroic in meeting great sorrows bravely. We sit at the feet of dark-browed trouble and are sweetened and strengthened by the lesson she reads us. Our wayward wills are disciplined, our ideals made luminous, and our ardor chastened. So that for what remains of life we are truer comrades and better Christians, but will the grace that is granted for special needs hold fast in the bewilderments of perplexed daily living? Will the aid that comes to guide us through deep waters condescend to tarry with us when only shoe-deep in brawling streams?

* * * * *

I think it will. The woman who stands rebellious before the wash tub, or aghast before the pile of dishes that three times a day, 365 days, for forty years, confront her, may gain consolation from the same source that supplies her when the baby dies, or hope dips into the sea like a sunken sun. I wish I could convince every tired and discouraged woman of this belief. It may seem to you that no human heart can know all you have to bear, that your burdens are heavier than ever yet were borne on human shoulders, and that there is no end to the drudgery, monotony, and pain of your existence. The husband who promised to bear your burdens is quite regardless of them now; your children have grown away from your yearning heart, and you have no time to nourish new friendships. You stand alone, your destiny marked out before you like a long and dusty road leading to the grave.

* * * * *

Not so, dear heart! There is one waiting to give you comfort. There is one waiting to lead you home. It is possible for Him to lighten your load and hang clusters on the bitter vine. Nobody else can. Nobody else would. Shall aught avail, then, to destroy the life that can claim so sympathizing a friend, so tender and all-comprehending a lover?

> If our love were but more simple,
> We should take Him at His word,
> And our lives would be all sunshine
> In the sweetness of our Lord!

If I am to kill a chicken (a thing I wouldn't do, my dear, for a thousand pounds!) I do not proceed to do the deed by cruel and protracted methods. I should be arrested by the Humane Society if I went to work to put poison in the doomed fowl's daily rations, or nip it slyly now and then with a redhot hatpin.

The cat that was killed by care suffered far more than the cat that perished by a quick bullet.

When a horse is disabled and unfit for service, the merciful man knocks it in the head with a well-aimed blow, and that's the last of it. But we have different ways of killing love, and trust, and kindly feeling in one another's hearts. We make use, all too often, of the North American Indian's original method of protracted torture. And love, and trust, and kindly feeling, although they die hard, and are a long time dying, under the process, are as certainly doomed as the chicken, the cat, and the disabled horse are by the blow of the hatchet, the sting of the bullet, or the crash of the club. There is many a home to-day where love is slowly dying under the torture inflicted by a sarcastic tongue, or where it already lies dead under the peculiar processes of this cowardly mode of torment. The drunkard's wife is not more to be pitied than the wife of the cold-blooded husband whose tongue holds the venom of a dozen serpents. I would rather be mated to a man who should throw a chair at me now and then than to such a husband as we see occasionally, who murders his wife's peace and happiness slowly yet surely from day to day with cruel and biting words of suspicion and contempt. I might dodge the chair, but I couldn't dodge the word, and, besides, bruises inflicted on the body heal under the application of liniment and arnica, but there has no salve been found yet to cure the hurt of a sarcastic tongue. There are many unhappy homes in the world, and many broken hearts, and there is a great cry raised against the causes therefor. A crusade is even being raised against the giant forces that combine to break up the harmony of domestic concord, yet the lesser influences for evil are ignored and forgotten. It is as though we armed ourselves to go out and shoot elephants in a country where rabbits were devastating the crops, or fitted out a fleet to catch whales in a fresh-water pond full of eels and catfish. Intemperance, and unfaithfulness, and all the greater causes of sorrow in the world's homes have always plenty of armed and steadfast opposers and foes, but the little hidden foxes that spoil the vines run to and fro without molestation.

It takes as much heroism often to sit down and endure for a half-hour the electric buzz-saw of a modern dentist as it takes to march to battle behind a drum and a flag; but whoever wrote a poem to the hero or heroine of the dentist's chair? It takes more Christian grace to live in the same house with a sarcastic tongue than to wear a hair-cloth shirt and do ante-sunrise penance, and yet who stops to say a word of comfort to the saint inured to domestic torment, or learn a lesson from her sublime patience and enduring courage? It is not going to be those who march up by and by and show saber cuts on the body who will be called heroes, but those who display scars made in the heart that were silently endured, who will wear the laurel and the bay. We all pride ourselves on the etiquette that teaches us to be gentlemen and ladies in the drawing-room or in public places, but when some of us have learned the etiquette that teaches us to be more gentlemanly and ladylike as fathers and mothers, sisters and brothers, parents and children, we shall have learned a new code. The man is a coward who is civil only where he dare not be otherwise, but becomes a bully behind the closed doors of his home. What we need is less mannerism for show, and more courtesy at home. You would never dare to speak to a lady in society, sir, as you speak to your wife and daughter, and I say you are the worst sort of a cad when you take a tone with the defenseless ones at home you would not dare assume to a stranger.

All politeness that is put on merely for show is like the stain the cabinetmaker puts on a pine board; politeness that amounts to anything is in the grain of the wood, not an external application. We make a terrible fuss when our growing children put a dinner knife to their lips, yet say nothing when they pester and harass one another with mean and sarcastic speeches until good nature flies out the window and evil temper stalks in at the door.

I will take my chance, any day, to live with the person who commits the solecism of putting his knife in his mouth rather than with the person who deals in anger-provoking speech and innuendo.

You take it greatly to heart when the slugs get into the roses, and your June gardens are despoiled of their sweetness and beauty. And yet there is something worse that gets into the home, that garden of delight, when unkind and sarcastic speech creeps in with its chilling blight. I have in my mind's eye as I write a family of growing sons and daughters more desolate

13

than any garden devoured by slugs or withered by devastating blight. The father sits over against everything that is spontaneous and ardent and earnest with his cold and clammy ridicule; the older boys emulate their father, and the girls are ashamed to be fresh and natural and enthusiastic, as they were meant to be, for fear of evoking laughter and contempt. In the midst sits the mother, a dear little frightened morsel of a woman, full of poetic fancies and immortal enthusiasms stifled and confined like so many infant Moseses in bullrush baskets, with Herod stalking up and down the bank.

If you must murder love then in the heart and home, wherein you ought to glorify and crown it, I pray you go out and get drunk, or rob a bank, or skip to Canada with a defaulter's grip-sack; anything, so that the deed is done quickly and poor innocent love be not a long time dying, like a victim on the rack.

I wish joy lasted as flies do. I wish that after the summer, with its beautiful, balmy weather, was ended, and the long, chill

evenings should close in about life's little
day, we might all of us sit down in the
warmth of pleasant memories and be buzzed
at by lively delights and nipped by sportive
fancies, as I am buzzed at and nipped to-
night by these abominable flies. There is
nothing in animate nature I so utterly de-
test as I do a familiar, inquisitive, noisy fly,
and yet, how the riotous insect outlasts
every other feature of the season. Roses
fade early, flowers of all sorts vanish with
the first blight of frost, birds fly away, the
orioles and the bluebirds, the cardinals and
the bobolinks, go trooping away southward
in long, wavering lines of animate shadow
before a flake has fallen or an icicle formed;
but the fly remains with us to partake of
Thanksgiving dinner. Each day beholds
its lively resurrection from the chill of the
preceding night. They survive as only sin
and sorrow survive, in a world that would
be all the fairer and more alluring for their
absence. Somebody told me the other day
to buy a certain powder and waft it at night
about the rooms especially infested by
flies, then close the doors and windows, hie
to bed, and the morning shall find the home
flyless. I bought the powder, wafted it,

went to bed. Awoke in the night dreaming that an elephant had casually sat down on my left lung, and that my right lung and other vitals had ossified. Thought I was asphyxiated by coal gas, but remembering that we burned wood, came to the conclusion that I had acute pneumonia. Roused the family and requested a poultice, but found every other member of the family prostrated. Suffered acutely until dawn, when we found the whole place shoe-deep with a yellow powder like the pollen of a tiger-lily, which reminded us of the experiment of the night before. Not a vivacious fly was injured, but the family struggled bravely back from death's doors and resolved to try no more experiments.

I wish I knew why people have to eat. Why couldn't we keep up steam by some other process than by munching bits of food like oxen, sheep and donkeys grazing in a pasture? There is nobody who looks the least bit interesting when masticating, or even in the premonitory stages of making a

selection. A man may be ever so kingly,
so heroic or so grand, or a woman ever so
beautiful, so charming or so lovable, but
the moment either begins to eat, down they
go to the level of the brute. I don't see
why nature didn't ordain that we should
feed the marvelous engine that keeps the
blood rushing through the veins by some
more economical and delicate process. A
poor man has to work so awfully hard and
a poor woman has to plan and putter so
constantly just to keep enough money in the
purse to maintain this humiliating necessity
of feeding. Among other things that the
evolution of the years shall bring to mankind shall be a process by which nutriment
shall be condensed so that a whole meal
shall lie in the compass of a pellet, and an
entire beef be compressed into a lozenge.
When our future great, great grandchildren
feel the pangs of unsatiated appetite they
will only have to take a sly little nibble behind their delicate handkerchiefs of a lozenge or a drop that shall contain the condensed nutriment of a full meal. No more
idiotic chewing and mouthing, no greedy
dabs at special tidbits, no consequent soil-
ing of fingers and lips or spoiling of pretty

gowns by carelessly spilled sauces and gravies. Won't it be jolly? And don't you wish you had been born a century later to have enjoyed it all?

I wish I knew why the woman has not yet been born who knows how to carry an umbrella. The most of them wield it like a battle-axe, or trail it like the banner in a lost cause, or carry it as a raw recruit carries a bayonet. I never get safely home after a rainstorm that I don't call the family together and sing a hymn of praise that I have been spared to meet them once more. I tell you there are pleasanter ways of dying than being pierced to the brain, or deprived of an eye, or impaled by a sharp umbrella stick. And if I must be bayoneted I would rather meet my fate on a battlefield than on a street-crossing, or on a windy corner where men congregate to gibe at my misery. I started out in life with many friends, but one by one a coldness has sprung up between us by reason of walking together in the rain, until the original number is sadly depleted. We have started to walk under the same umbrella, and conversations of the following nature have only stopped this side of blows:

"Can't you carry that umbrella a little steadier?"

"Look out! You are knocking my hat over my eyes."

"Great heavens! Do you want to put out my eyes?"

"Really, I must request you to hold that thing further on your own side; you have pulled half the hair off my scalp already."

"You are too idiotic to walk straight, much less to carry an umbrella. I think I will get along better alone."

And so we have parted, to meet no more as we have met in happier days.

I wish I knew why the most prayerful and pious parents have such bad children as a rule, and vice versa. I had a cousin, three removed, who went as a missionary to India. She returned after many years to place two fatherless babes in school. Two such diabolical imps never flitted across the vision of my mortal dream. They bit and glowered like little demons, and those of us who belonged to the same blood, but were not missionaries, used to brood over our own little ones when those two boys were around, as a hen broods over her flock when the hawk is in the sky. I have a neighbor who goes to prayer-meeting two evenings in the week, and belongs to the Village Aid, and the Foreign Mission and the King's Daughters, and her children will steal potatoes out of the grocer's basket when they can't get apples. I wonder if some day these freaks of heredity shall all be accounted for and we shall know just why the Lord gave pickles when we ex-pected plums, and caused the wild juniper tree to bring forth fruit, and the sheltered strawberry plant to yield nothing but leaves.

I wonder if there is a spot left in all the world where one could be alone and not be bothered by folks. Take the wings of the air and fly away to the most distant heart of the loveliest hill and ten to one the first

thing your foot treads upon will be a pea-
nut-shell, a sign positive that some free-born
citizen has been there before you. Go to
the sea and cast yourself prone upon its silver sands; watch the tumbling surf and imagine that there is nothing left in all the
world but you and the gray sea-gull that
poises like a winged thought between the
billows and the blue air, but the sudden
cackle of a shallow wit's laugh, or the fuss
and flurry of some feather-head passing by,
will dispel your dream of solitude before it
is fully begun. I ran away from town the
other day in search of a place to interview
my own self and find out how the times
were faring with that part of me destined,
I humbly hope, to outlast the needs of bread
and butter, dress fabrics and shoe leather.
But do you suppose I found it? We
stopped for a half-day at Niagara, and I
clambered away down the river bank and
found a place so sheltered and so beautiful
that I almost hoped the realization of my
wildest dream had found fulfillment. Far
above my head the world seemed full of
falling water and emerald sheen and rainbow-tinted sheets of spray, where the great
fall poised upon its rocky verge. At my

feet in wild commotion and angry unrest
the breakers rushed and bounded between
the narrow confines of the pass. Ever since
the stars swung into place to light a newly-
created earth upon its way; before a human
voice had waked the echoes of the primal
morning, or a human foot trod the verdure
of the fresh young world, these furious torrents have kept up their ceaseless wage of
war. The ocean has its times of rest and
calm, when a shallop made of rose leaves
might float secure upon its breathless tides,
but Niagara's torment is never done. It is
always lashed and torn in eternal conflict,
and still will be when you and I, with our
headaches and our fears, have been blown
about within the infinite spaces of the stars
ten thousand years. Just as I was indulg-
ing in these thoughts and feeling throughout each fiber of my happy soul that it was
well to be alone with nature at her grandest
and her best, I heard voices on the ledge
six feet or less from where I sat. "Have
you got any gum?" "Not a bit." "Oh,
pshaw; I'm just dying for some." As a
mower scatters clover heads, or as a stiff
breeze carries away dandelion disks, so flew
to the windward my happy fancies of soli-

tude as I gathered myself together and rode up the incline, priced the bead baskets and reviled the moccasin to my heart's content along with the gum-chewing crowd.

There is not much enjoyment to be gotten out of a trip on an elevated train through the heart of New York, but there is a wonderful chance to study life in its varying phases. Starting from the Battery and traveling ten miles north as the bird flies, one gets glimpses of people and things undreamed of by the tourist afoot. In a shabby chamber behold a tired sewing-girl making shirts. As the train rumbles by she does not even lift the lashes from her pale cheek to watch its progress. Her stint must be accomplished or the slender pittance upon which she depends to hold at bay the two wolves of want and dishonor is no longer hers. In another room a little child lies sick upon a comfortless cot. The long bright hair is tossed aside upon a pillow that seems none too clean, and the little hands are partly folded underneath a cheek sadly wan and pale. A moment we watch

the flying picture and then it changes to an
upper room in a lodging house, full of men
playing cards and drinking beer. Their
ribald songs float in at the window as we
roll by. The next scene that unfolds with
kaleidoscopic effect is a costumer's room
hung with masks and gay dresses. A pretty
girl is selecting a domino, and stops to flirt
with the conductor as we flash by. Another room discovered what is apparently a
thief at work. He seems to be forcing the
lock of a trunk, and is so intent he does not
notice our passing. In a window of a tenement that overlooks a dingy street a woman
is leaning out upon her folded arms, and as
we pass we hear her curse a little child that
is pulling at her dress. Two lovers are
whispering together in a doorway, while an
irate old woman bears down upon them
from the hallway bent on mischief. Why
can't old folks stay out of scenes like this?
There is no harm in a stolen word or two
when hearts are callow and hope is young.
A hideous old Jew is crouching over a dirty
bundle in a dimly-lighted room. We wonder if he is another Fagin, and almost think
he is when we see a couple of boys shrink-
ing against the further wall. A pretty

young woman is crooning her baby to sleep
in another chamber, and no princess was
ever cradled in more loving arms. A cat
is stealing meat from off a scanty table
while the good housewife's back is turned,
a bird is hopping in a cage that hangs in an
open window, a rose is blooming in a pot
that stands upon a neat little shelf, above
which a curly-headed boy is poising dangerously near the window ledge. Somebody
is quarreling in a room as we glide on into
the shadow. Somebody is playing on an
old cracked piano in another, and our ears
catch the notes of "Annie Rooney" trolled
forth by an excellent tenor. Our ride is
ended and over long before the memory of
all that we have seen has left the mazes of
our brain. God pity us all as we go our
various ways in the world, for be we rich or
poor, dwell we in tenement or mansion, be
the heart within our bosom fresh and gay .
or sordid and withered and old, we have
much need of His constant care and His
patient love.

Lamb wrote once most quaintly about
the "Decay of Begging." I follow him

later and most unworthily, but neverthe-
less most earnestly, with a brief word on the
decay of courtesy. We are a bright generation and a progressive people. We ac-
cumulate and build up and increase, and
yet we have deteriorated wondrously in
good manners. It has come to be that if
a man is a thorough gentleman as to speech
and linen and conduct he is a "dude," and
if a woman stands aside to do a service in
a crowded street, such as to remove a
banana-skin, or lend her arm to a crippled
wayfarer, she is a "crank." We push, and
hustle, and elbow our way along towards
success, mindful only of number one, and
may the old boy take the hindmost. It is
an age of such everlasting and almighty
equality that the lower classes in seeking to
impress you with the fact that they are "as
good as you are," forget how to serve and
remember only to be insolent. In business
the gruffer, and grumpier, and more
brusque a man can be the more adaptation
he shows for his position. Magnates of
every kind are autocrats, and in many instances it were far safer to pull a lion's tail
than seek to be on terms of even flesh and
blood equality with an editor, a hotel clerk

or the young man at the theater ticket-win-
dow. For my part, I am dying to see the
world swing back, if need be, in its orbit,
and give us old-fashioned politeness towards all, reverence for the aged and courtesy and kind feeling from all to all.

I am told that the gods fell into a dispute
one day as to which of the four seasons was
the favorite of mankind. Seeing no other
way to bring peace from out the babble of
tongues, Jove commanded that each season
produce a masterpiece and present the same
to a quorum of the gods.

First, Spring evolved a day that shim-
mered like an opal through rosy mists and
low-lying clouds, tinted like the plumage of
a gray dove. And she bordered it with pale
violets that deepened as they grew, until
they showed the purple of King Solomon's
robes. And she scattered it all over with
touches of green, like up-springing grass by
loosened water courses, and sprays of blossoms, like snow when the sunshine finds
it. And she gave it the voice of a wood-
thrush in the twilight and drew over it a

veil of silver rain, shot through and through with broken rainbows and sunflashes.

* * * * *

Then Summer brought a day of golden calm, about whose brow were languid poppies and blue cornflowers steeped in sunshine. And a veil like the haze on far hills enveloped it, and its voice was the noonday note of the cushat dove, hid deep in fields of snowy buckwheat. And the hum of its drowsy bees was like the lullaby song that mothers sing to their sleepy children, while above it, like a butterfly that poises above a yellow rose, was the infinite peace of a cloudless heaven.

* * * * *

Next, Autumn poured a crystal goblet high with wine and placed it in the hands of a day that laughed like a beautiful woman and wore amethysts and topaz and great shining rubies at its throat. And the breath of this day made all the earth glad, so that it drank the wine of grapes and summoned the winds of heaven to smite their harps for joy. And its voice was like the voice of silver bugles when brave men march to war or the mellow notes of trumpets when conquerors return unto their homes.

* * * * *

Lastly, Winter laid at the feet of the gods a fair, dead day, whose loveliness was like the loveliness of a bride whom death hath taken. Its shroud was like the inner heart of milk weed when rosy-fingered children first unfold it, and about its brows were wrapped frost lace finer than cobwebs in the light of a wan moon. A single diamond blazed upon its breast, and in its pale and quiet hands was loosely wreathed a strand of priceless pearls.

* * * * *

And the gods, being much together, were bewildered with the masterpieces of each season's handiwork, and could make no choice. So they ordered that, while time endured, these perfect tests of seasonable weather should be perpetuated for the benefit of the sons and daughters of earth, and that somewhere within the round of the year should fall four absolutely perfect days. Who shall say that the past month did not bring in autumn's masterpiece somewhere

14

within the last quarter of its calendared days?

The other evening I was riding home on the suburban train. Near me sat a fat youth with less intelligence in his make-up than a biscuit has spice. He was known to me personally as shady both in morals and intellect. And what do you think the boy was reading?—"Prue and I!" No less than that, the sweetest, tenderest creation ever penned by a dreamer's fancy. Thinking that it would be of interest to find out how such a pearl came to be cast in the way of a rover such as he, I drew near and asked the question:

"What are you reading?"

"Oh, a novel I picked up; I liked the title, but I guess it's pretty slow."

"Do you think you ought to read erotic literature at your age?" I asked him.

After I had explained to him what "erotic" meant he answered, "I guess it won't hurt me, I've read pretty wild books in my time. If I find this is too-too, I'll not leave it around where the women folks will find it!"

I didn't stop laughing all the way home, but after all it made me mad. It all comes of this hodge-podge in literary mention. If you serve everything with the same sauce, who is to know fish from fowl? If you do not deal with intelligent clerks what is to help the classification of "Prue and I" with erotic slush, and who is to prevent the jumble? Perhaps you think a clean book might work reform in the reader who had fallen upon it through error, but if so you are mistaken. A rat can never be taught to eat cheese with a fork, nor can a depraved taste be taught the usages of refinement. No harm was done by the fool's reading the book of airy dreams; his possessing it was simply a desecration, as it would be to give a monkey the image of the Madonna to play with. The helter-skelter of book distribution would not occur were the distinction more reliable.

And what is true of books is true of people. We all pose in conglomerate. There are no individual distinctions, unless it be good clothes. If the Magdalene wears rags we avoid her; if she wears seal-skin and diamonds we accept her invitation to lunch.

"She is a splendid woman," somebody

says of the person who lives in the next flat. Why is she splendid? How does the sumptuous term fit? Is she brainy? Is she brave? Is she big-hearted? Is she tender both in thought and manner? Is she brilliant? Is she a champion of losing causes and diffident people? Is she wide in her outlooks and generous with her money? Not at all. Then why does she pass with the testimonial card of "splendid" tacked to her mantle? Merely because she moves in the best society, gives elegant dinners, wears a winning surface smile, possesses tactful manners and can out-dress the Queen of Sheba? That makes her splendid, does it? And we apply the same term to the heroism of the noble Six Hundred, to the devotion of Jeanne d'Arc to principle, to the courage of a soldier in battle, and to the sacrifice on Calvary. Out on your false labels then, either on fruit or people!

Another friend is gone. Not to heaven, perhaps, but out into the white mist of silence that envelops the world. Noiselessly as bubbles burst or sunshine leaves the hills they are passing away, these tried and trusted friends of earth, and day is not more sure to fade into night nor stars to pale before the flush of dawn than is the certainty of their departure from our firesides and our hearts. To-day it is a mother who hears the chiming of the golden bells across the misty sea and fearlessly enters the phantom bark that carries her to the thither shore. In vain her children reach out their eager hands to bid her stay, in vain their plaintive voices call her back; the silvery fog receives her and her dear name becomes but a sanctified memory within our home.

Again, it is the dimpled baby that feels the soft enfolding of angel arms that carry him beyond the misty breakers. Gently as a shadow rests upon a white rose fall the fringes of his fading eyes; softly as a summer wind dies among the flowers vanishes his fluttering breath from off the breast where we, with tears, so closely held him! He is gone, and the silent mist receives him, too, as sunrise receives a fading star. A trusty servant is dead. Hearing a summons more imperative than ours could ever be, the faithful hands lay by their task, the willing feet tarry while yet the errand is unaccomplished, and out into the gray shadow passes a heart that was ever true and a love that was both loyal and incorruptible. And now "old Blaze" is gone. Twelve years he lived with us. He had been more faithful than many friends. He had been more willing than many lovers. He had served us as steadily in storm as in sunshine, and never rebelled when duty called him to face the icicle blast or the driving snow. People have said to us: "You do unwisely to trust old Blaze so implicitly! Age is not always steadiness, nor do years insure reliability; he will do mischief yet." But he never abused our confidence, nor failed us in the trust confided to his care. Bravely and unweariedly he carried our hearts' treasures, a load of laughing children, through the wooded drives and all along the bluffs of our summer home. He held his glossy head high and curved his shining neck with pride, feeling with almost human intelligence the responsibilities placed upon him. The other day poor Blaze was sick. He trembled like a leaf and refused to eat. His eyes sought ours with almost human pleading for relief. We gave him what remedies we could and left him at night with a farewell

touch on his slender nose of encouragement
and cheer. To-morrow, we thought, old
Blaze would be himself again. To-morrow
came, and found him dead among the with-
ering grasses of the pasture that had been
his summer home. The head which had
ever been held so high at our approach was
low; the eye that had never failed in its welcome was unheedful. Poor, faithful old
Blaze! here's to your memory. May the
record of your faithful service endure forever in our hearts. May the lesson of an
unfailing devotion teach us a new loyalty to
our friends. May the memory of your endurance make us brave and the recollection
of your docility make us kind. And when
your fleet limbs are in the grave and a new
horse stands in the harness may the children, remembering you, be kinder to every
dumb animal, slower to deeds of heedless
cruelty toward any of God's creatures to
whom he has given almost human powers
of affection, but denied the power of speech.

The doctor has ordered me a rest, evidently expecting it to be served like a plate

of hot cakes. All I am supposed to do is to recline on a couch and say to Providence: "Please bring me a rest medium rare and without gravy." That is the way we order beef, my dear, but the same methods do not apply to bodily and mental recuperation. I should like to append a diary of the few days I have been spending at home resting(?).

Monday—Thought I would sleep late, but was so accustomed to rising before sunrise that I yielded to the force of habit and was up at 5:30. As the girl had been out all night to a dance and was feeling tired thought I would get breakfast. Spent the morning looking over closets and tinkering loose door-knobs. In the afternoon seated the boy's knickerbockers and sewed on nineteen dozen shoe buttons. Went to bed at 11, after spending the evening cleaning out the stove to rid the room of coal-gas.

Tuesday—Cleaned woodshed.

Wednesday—Took up the sitting-room carpet and helped wash paint.

Thursday—Girl's day out and had company to tea. In the evening upholstered the old lounge.

Friday—The whole family down with the

grip. Made toast for seven invalids and squeezed lemons for drink. Removed cans from back yard and set out slips.

Saturday—Girl left. Took her place in kitchen. Family still ill and demands for toast alternated with cries for gruel. Washed seven thousand dishes and baked bread.

Sunday—Pump gave out. Spent the morning hauling buckets out of a deep cistern. To-day is Monday and the prospects are good for doing the family wash, as every washerwoman within a radius of three miles is dying with the grip. At this pace of recuperation by the end of another week I shall be in Rose Hill. Out of all this arises the old question the poet asked of the winds, the moon and the sea, "Where shall rest be found?" Nowhere, my dear, this side the little plat of ground that is getting ready to bring out its crop of April grasses and May buttercups, where you and I some day shall sleep the happy years away.

CHAPTER V.

I never hear the term "old maid" but what something within me stirs like a tiger thirsting for gore. When it shall be a reproach for green apples to ripen, for buds to blow and for May to orb into June, then it shall be a disgrace for girls to grow to be old. And when you find me a married woman who is never cranky and odd and queer, then you may say that it is a blight upon a girl's life to be unmated. There are not many women who have not had the opportunity to marry if they would. Look about you and count the unhappy wives who would be unmarried if they could. Mated to a clown, a tyrant or a knave, they spend their lives in turmoil, and yet mark how they join in the jest and sneer at the expense of the "old maid." All glory to the woman who is independent enough to wear the badge of spinsterhood rather than marry for a home, and the tenderest reverence for the woman who remains faithful to a grave

and flaunts no flower of second love above
it.

It is all very well for "Mary" while youth
dashes her cheek with crimson, and lights
her eyes with the sparkle of its elixir, while
her father is prosperous and the old roof-
tree stands safe above her head. Life has
no more difficult problem than the selection
of a bonnet or the matching of a shade.
Friends congregate around like swallows on
the eaves of a gambrel roof, and the years
stretch before her like the vista of a sun-
lighted boulevard. But one day Mary
awakens to the fact that girlhood has departed, younger sisters have grown to mat-
ronly years, school friends are young mothers, and the family record points away back
into the mists of antiquity to date her birth.
What shall she do now? Shall she enter
into a contract with a man for whom she
does not care a rap, to sew on buttons and
keep house in exchange for his name and
convoy? Being a brainy, sensible woman,
Mary passes over her last chance, such as it
is, and emerges alone from the shadowy
and music-haunted woods of youth into the
companionless sweep and uneventful desert
of middle life.

Fathers have a trick of dying, and mothers as well, leaving elderly daughters doubly alone in the world. One by one the shingles in the old roof-tree crumble and Mary is by and by left homeless and alone in the world. The children of her prosperous brothers and sisters love her and long to hear her tell them stories and make shadow-pictures for them in the firelight as she flits from home to home for longer and longer tarryings. She earns her right to a shelter and a home by darning stockings, patching rents, rocking cradles and nursing the sick. If little Johnny takes the fever Aunt Mary tends him. When baby dies Aunt Mary folds white buds in the waxen hands and drops the last tear on its quiet face. When the girls are married Aunt Mary gives the parting pat to bridal fixings and is the mother's rival in the bride's fond love. She merges her identity in the well-being of those who love her and for whom she lives. Patiently she plods along her uneventful way, finding her religion in every-day duties well performed, her rights in just the service heaven has ordained for her, easing others' burdens, dusting parlors, sweeping rooms or making beds, with brave, reliant heart, accepting each span of the way unquestioning.

She always has a word of sympathy for young folks and their escapades. When a pitcher is broken or a vase shattered by careless hands Aunt Mary shoulders the responsibility to save the young ones from a scolding. She may fret a bit now and then, but what of that? Do not the married sisters do the same? At last one day "Aunt Mary" dies. Faded and careworn and old she lies before us. Feebly her fingers grope for the touch of the hands she has held so often between her patient palms. The eyes that have never mirrored themselves in the eyes of children of her own kindle with a light we never before beheld in their serene depths. With a prayer on her lips for our welfare, with a backward glance of abiding love for us, she slips away and the shadows veil her from our sight forever. What angel bands come down to greet her, what radiant crown is granted and what sweet benediction of peace is hers we cannot tell. But this we know, that dear, queer, unselfish, simplehearted Aunt Mary shall take precedence over many who called her "old maid" here. For God is no respecter of persons, and "they who know my will and do it" shall shine yonder when the fair and the learned and the wise are forgotten.

I met a friend the other morning on the cars. He looked so thin and suspiciously bright of eye that I was on the point of exclaiming as to his appearance, when he fortunately interrupted me with this remark: "Amber, I have a topic for you."

Assuring him that topics were what I was after, he proceeded as follows:

"I wish you would write up the busy-bodies who are always telling a fellow how badly be looks. (Oh, how I shook hands with myself.) Every old lady I meet lately has something to say about how thin I am, until I hardly care to ride outside the smoking car on my way to town."

After all, there is a good bit of justice in my friend's complaint. It is not pleasant to be told that one looks ill, that the flesh is fading from the bones and (by implication) that one is on the quarter-stretch of life's race-track. Such communications are

about as soothing as the remarks of an onlooker might be, who, seeing our boat
adrift in the rapids above Niagara, should
bawl from the band: "Hi! young fellow,
you're going over the falls!" "Say, my
friend, you'll be drowned in another minute!" Knowing your condition yourself
would be bad enough, but to have it roared
at you by the lusty rustic would make you
feel like coming back from the other world
to punch his head.   If we cannot find something cheery to say to one another when we
meet let us keep silence, as the Friends do,
and wait for the spirit to send us a glimmer
of sense.

I read a story once about a certain king's
son who wandered through his father's
country bearing a flask of royal wine and
beseeching those whom he met to quench
their thirst. Some refused, being slow to
perceive, through the disguise that he wore,
that their would-be benefactor was of kingly
birth. Some laughed the proffered wine to
scorn and would none of it, preferring rather
to drink stale beer. Some tasted, and slyly

spat it out, not liking the flavor. In all the land there was not found one to drain the cup, or thank the giver, although the wine he carried was of royal vintage, and about his brows wavered the softened shadow of a crown. That, thought I to myself, is a fit representation of the disadvantages of superiority in a sordid world. Better keep your flask corked tight than waste its aroma upon those who prefer cheap beer. Consort with your own kind and drink together of the special nectar the gods pour for you, but do not hope to educate the tastes of such as were born without perception of the finer flavors. Though you bray a fool, yet shall his folly not depart from him, and although you offer wine all day to a donkey, he will turn from you to quench his thirst in a wayside pool.

Of what avail is all the reform work in the world against the power of evil and the coronation of sin? A few women work together to crush the head of the old whisky serpent under their heel. What do they accomplish in a country where immigration and evil heredity, with the right to propagate a miserable species, have it their own way? If you and I were to go out and seek to purify the waters of our own vile-smelling river by sprinkling cologne into it, we should be doing just about as telling work as the well-meaning reformers are doing against the progress of evil in the land.

It is slow work waiting for the summer to get rid of its weeds; waiting for the bats to fly away and give place to singing birds; waiting for the clouds to roll by and let in the shining of steady blue weather. But God's time is some time, and though you and I may be dead and gone to dust a thousand years before it comes to pass, some day there will be nothing to drink but the King's wine, and no thirst remaining but such as it can assuage.

Somebody is really talking of establishing a colony on some distant island of the sea, where an attempt shall be made to rear a race of unblemished and sin-untampered
15

souls.　Given a hundred orphaned babies, with the surety that they are not direct descendants of habitual criminals, and nurture them in absolute cleanliness both physically and morally, and I do not see why the product might not be like the fruitage of a well-cared-for, pruned and grafted apple-tree.　The little ones are to be brought to years of maturity with absolutely no knowledge of vice or the appliances by which vice feeds and multiplies in the world.　Whisky, tobacco, cards, everything that tends to the downfall of man from his primal estate (how about women?) are to be absolutely tabooed. At a marriageable age these sheltered lambs are to be allowed to choose mates among themselves, and who shall say what beautiful results shall begin to brighten and bloom by about the fourth generation?　I declare, if I had no prior ties I would engage myself to go out with that colony as head nurse. I can imagine nothing better, without it might be to die and go direct to the angels.

I was born under an evil star.　Luck has always been against me.　For instance, if

the looms of America turn out one fabric
more desperately shoddy than another I am
sure to get it for a dress pattern. If the
hens of this great and fine country conspire
together to impose an especially stale egg
upon the market, I am the one who joyous-
ly undertakes to break that egg into the pot
of morning coffee. And so it is not to be
wondered at that I had hardly touched the
pillow, on my memorable ride through
Central New York, when the conductor discovered that there was something wrong
with my ticket. I spent the night in seeking to convince relays of New York Central
railway officials that I was not an imposter.
I never knew how hard it was to prove
respectability. Somehow one gets used to
the fact that one is honest and of good re-
pute, just as one gets used to the fact that
one is white or able-bodied, and any doubt
thrown upon the self-evident fact is a blow.
I knew in the face of all compromising circumstances that I came honestly by the
ticket which caused so much excitement in
the liveried bosom of the various conductors, but I had no means of convincing them
of the fact. Consequently my entire journey
until the end of the route was passed in vain

and baffling disputations. But it takes discipline to bring out the character, just as it takes storms to season timber, and I trust those conductors are chastened and better men for having met me and my ticket.

Good nature is an excellent attribute, and for domestic use cannot be surpassed by any one of the Christian graces. But too much good nature is apt to make a person appear like a half-wit. It is one thing to be amiable, and another thing to be stupid; blessed be he or she who in this as in other things, finds the golden mean. To stand around with your eyes like china saucers and invite people to insult you and impose upon you, just to show off your sweet disposition, savors a little too much of the disposition of the imbecile hen or the woolly sheep to suit me. If there is any of the human in your make-up (and a man or woman without it might as well be without a spine!) the temptation to pitch in and get even with the boor who insults you, or with the rogue who seeks to outwit you, is too

strong to be resisted. To treat a certain
class of people with "silent contempt" is too
much like seeking to calm a mad dog by
the music of flutes. A shotgun would be
more effectual. Flutes and dignity are well
enough for summer eves and for lovers and
poets; but when you come to deal with
brutes and boors clubs and self-assertion
will do the business better.

One of the experiments of Thanksgiving
day just passed, in a certain little home
where there is more love than gold, was to
try and act as though certain it was the last
Thanksgiving day to be spent together as an
individual family. And it was a great success. Several times there was a good chance
for a quarrel, but the proposed thought put
a quietus on every tongue. Grandma found
herself handed about from place to place,
like a venerable queen under special escort.
The cushions were adjusted, and the foot-
stool brought without a murmur, and when
it came time for the dear old head to seek
its pillow, the whispered word in some-

body's ear that "it had been the pleasant-
est day she had spent for a great many
years" proved the success of the experiment
so far as grandma was concerned. And
that member of the little band who is always
"spoiling for a fight," as the boys say, who
goes around breathing flame, as it were, and
to whom the very stones in the street cry
aloud for vengeance, was so beautifully held
in check that long before night she had
beaten the record of all previous good be-
havior. It is a good thing, my dear, once
in a while to face this "last time" business.
There is a last time for everything on its way
for you and for me. There will be a last
time to awake in the morning, a last time to
go to business, a last time to read the daily
paper, a last time to say good-morning and
good-by. There will be a last time to speak
a loving word to the wife, or the child, or
the husband, a last time to be cross and dis-
obliging, a last time to be courteous and
sweet. There will be a last time to light
the evening lamp and a last time to ex-
tinguish it, a last time to disrobe the tired
body and a last time to fall asleep on earth.
Don't you think, in face of this thought, it
behooves us to occasionally compose our-

selves as though the last opportunity to be true and brave and strong and pure had reached us? Were to-day our last day on earth, I wonder if we would worry much about how our dress was going to fit or whether or no we would be invited to somebody's big reception. I wonder if envy or ambition or hatred or any such thing would linger another moment in our hearts. I think not, my dear, I think not.

How strange it is that street car corporations put so few men, comparatively, to work. There are lay figures who ride up and down, automatons who pull straps and gather in fares, but when it comes to men they are rare. The other evening I was riding on a certain grip. A modest young woman near me in clear and audible tones requested to be put off at Caramel street. The conductor stopped the car for her four blocks beyond, at Gingerbread avenue. A meek protest on her part was met by ducal silence and royal reserve. I wanted to say to her, "Dear child, be happy that It let you off at all! Bless your stars, my sweet maid, that It did not carry you clear through to the end of the route!" Another time, having the innocent purpose in my heart of catching a train, I asked a conductor how long it took to go to the end of the route. "Half an hour from here," replies my brave bird. So I settled back in my seat content. After the lapse of forty-five minutes I mildly asked why I had not been given the correct information at first, so that I might have sought other and swifter means of conveyance. Do you think I got any answer? Does the unweaned babe get an answer when it questions the distant moon? The desire to shed the blood of the menial who had made me lose my train was so strong upon me that I left the car hurriedly and said my prayers all the way over to the depot. Don't blame the officials for all the outrages imposed upon the public. Put the blame where, five out of every seven times, it belongs, with the putty men who run the cars.

Sailing into harbor comes the old weather-beaten craft again. The lettering on its

side bespeaks good cheer, but the command
of the ship has long been usurped by a
pirate crew, largely made up of carking
cares and dark debts and deep anxieties.
We used to go out on the headlands and
toss our caps when we saw old "Christmas"
in the offing, but of late years we are more
apt to sneak out behind the house to weep
over our poor little emptied pocketbooks
and hide ourselves from the righteous demands of the butcher and the baker, whose
claims have been ignored and set aside that
we might pay tribute to an extortionate
Christmas. The days of small gifts, with
love to prompt them, have long gone by,
and competition has its clutch upon the
throat of even the Lord's natal day.

I think it was the great Goethe who said
that a man could always be judged by what
made him laugh. Whether the utterance of
Goethe or of plain John Smith, it is the utterance of profound wisdom. I am willing,
for my part, to choose my friend, be that
friend man or woman, by the test above

mentioned. I may make a mistake if I attempt to gauge him by the church he attends, the coat he wears, or the language he uses, but I shall be pretty sure of a correct estimate if I watch for what amuses him. The man who laughs at the moral downfall of his brother man is a human ghoul. I think I should find a hospital ward quite as humorous a place as the scene of a fellow-creature's mastery by temptation. When the poor, half-crazy inebriate reels by, with his whisky-inflamed brain, it may perhaps be a sight to make devils laugh with exultation, but the men and women who find the spectacle a merry one are not the sort I care to cultivate.

The laugh that is expended on the minister when he falls from his high estate, or the defaulter when he skips with his boodle, or the woman when she shames her sex by misconduct, is not the laughter that proves a good heart and a pure conscience. It is, to other laughter, what the hyena's grin is to the smile of the June morning, or the screech of a night-hawk to the carol of a lark. If I see a boy in school laughing when another is punished, I do not need a prophet to tell me what sort of a man that boy will make. The malicious spirit within him will work out its own harvest just as the seeds of thistles sprout prickly fruit.

The mirth that is invoked by the discomfiture of others is the index of a low mind. It is a common thing to hear a boisterous laugh when a poor unfortunate falls headlong on the icy pavement, or stumbles over a bit of rumpled carpet and measures his length before a roomful of guests, but to my thinking such laughter is the outcome of ill breeding and a hard heart.

It does not need protracted blowing to yield the sound of a trumpet, the first blast is enough; and it does not require long acquaintance with a man to find out what material he is made of. Open laughter at the embarrassment of another is a certain test that the metal is poor.

Merry, heartfelt laughter is a great sweetener of life, but, like good coffee, it must be well cleared of the grounds of ill will and contain no deleterious admixture of common chickory. There is nothing on earth more delightful to listen to than witty laughter, and nothing more tormenting than the silly and causeless cachination of fools. Between a laugh and a giggle there is the

width of the horizon. I could sit all day
and listen to the heartsome ha! ha! of a
couple of bright and jolly men, but would
rather be shot with a Winchester rifle, at
short range, than be forced to listen to the
te! he! of a pair of ill-natured or silly gossips.
A really wicked man seldom laugh's. Humor is not the gift of the cruel or the im-
·pure, and humor of the genuine sort is next
to the divine attribute in any nature. A
person who has a real "Dickensy" sense of
humor will not usually laugh at the wrong
thing. A smutty story has no charm for
such. Vice and impurity cannot thrive
under the open and mellow influence of a
genial and humorous nature. And also the
men and women endowed with this choice
attribute are loth to do an unkind deed to
either a fellow creature or the most insignificant brute. They will step out of their
way to avoid crushing a toiling ant, and
their tears for others' ills are quite as ready
as their laughter for others' weal.

Cultivate that part of your nature, then,
that helps you see the bright and mirth-
some side of life. So shall you be enabled
to shed many of life's troubles, as the plumage of the bird sheds the rain. But discour-

age all tendencies to find amusement in anything that is harsh or uncharitable, or impure, and thus do your mite towards ridding the world of many of its thorns and weeds, planting velvet-leaved pansies of loving and happy thoughts instead.

There are more bondages than the bondage of sin. Bad habits are not the only chains that proclaim a state of servitude. Take the conformist, the person who is afraid to take a single step in life without first stopping to question what people are going to say about it. No old African slave in dread of the lash was ever under more cruel bondage. Take the case of good old Mr. Smith. His health demands ale, or beer, perhaps. He is afraid to buy it for fear the neighbors will see the bottles delivered. He is afraid to drink it at a restaurant for fear somebody will see him. He is afraid to show a little common sense and tone up his own body, taking the responsibility upon his soul, because he is a slave to the idle opinion of folks who don't care a snap what he does with himself, and who will dismiss his case lightly, as a bee dismisses a buckwheat blossom when it has extracted the last drop of honey. Gossip is the honey that stocks the hives of human bees. If Mr. Smith would argue this or any other question out with his conscience and his God (if he owns either) and act upon a fair understanding with either or both, regardless of popular opinion, he would no longer be a slave, but a free man with the glorious privilege suddenly cast before him of being independent. Take the slave to punctuality. I would rather dwell with a wild man of the woods than spend my days with the lunatic whose whole existence hinges upon a time-card. It doesn't particularly matter whether he takes the 8 o'clock train or the one ten minutes later, but do you suppose anything short of sudden death would keep him from that special train? What if you do get left once in a while? It is not a matter of eternal salvation with you, is it? Of course, it is well to be prompt, but there are circumstances to modify even punctuality, and I believe in asserting independence once in a while, rather than be chained to a dial-plate.

"Come, hurry up!" pipes the punctual bird, "we shall be late!" And things go with a whew; breakfast with a bang, and family prayers by steam, to serve no other earthly purpose than to keep that man's time-serving record clean. And the tired woman, she who is under bondage to the legend of stereotyped housekeeping. It is summer weather, perhaps, and nobody sits in the parlor. Everybody chooses the piazzas and the hammocks, but do you suppose this slave to housekeepers' custom failed to sweep on Friday? Her windows must be cleaned bi-weekly, her silver polished, and a lot of other non-essentials attended to, sink or swim, live or die! Why? Because she is a slave to non-essentials, and wants to keep the chains rubbed bright. If tired women would regulate matters with a little more regard for comfort, and less for custom, life would take on serener aspects.

Hark, how the winds are abroad to-night! Sit back in your comfortable chair, while the woodbine shadows flicker on the wall,

and no sound save the measured ticking of
the clock breaks the stillness of your quiet
room. Fold your hands listlessly, and let
the tired eyelids rest upon your tired eyes
awhile. You and I will never grow too old
I am thinking, to dream our dreams, to
build our castles, or muse upon the meaning of the restless voices of the wind. What
is the language to-night of these hurrying
hosts that fill the sky? They tell of swirling
wastes of billow, and stranded wrecks; of
ships sucked down like straws beneath a
yeasty sea; of white hands flung up in un-
noted appeal; of gleaming brows touched
by the fitful moonlight—one moment seen,
then gone forever; of sea-gulls beating
wearied breasts against high lonely towers
of cliff; of ragged headlands and booming
breakers; of mountain passes, where Nature
tones her thunder, harp of pines; of lonely
summits where the eagle builds her nest,
and shuddering torrents leap strong-footed
to the vales; of grand forests, and lonesome
haunts that foot of man has never trod; of
tireless prairies and sweeps of hill-girt plain;
of lonely graves and headstones fretted with
the dim splendor of the wind-hurried moon

—but positively, my dear, this is not cheerful; let's light the lamp, and chat awhile.

Did you ever test the beatitudes of country living? Did you ever own a garden patch and cultivate a cow? Did you ever go mad on chickens, and expend a fortune on fancy stock? I used to think that to live in the country was only a round or two from the acme of human bliss. I imagined that milk, set away in gleaming pans, by some secret influence of the stars resolved itself into golden pats of butter, stamped with a full blown rose, and ready for use. I fondly believed that cheese was a spontaneous growth—that eggs lay about loose like posies in a flower bed, that chickens in their juicy prime walked, ready dressed, to the dinner pot, and bullocks and fatling lambs laid themselves gently down in choice steaks and ruby chops ready for the eating. The heaviest cares of a country house-wife, I thought, were feeding fluffy chickens, and weeding flower beds. It came to pass in the delirium of house-hunting, a certain man proposed renting a suburban home for the season. There was a sound of revelry by night—packing trunks! A caravan wended its way out of the city gates—'twas the

16

household of Isaac headed for rustic meads.
And here we are, all that is left of us. What
with running to catch the early trains, the
head of the family has already scattered
twenty pounds of flesh to the winds. The
family heir has only been chased nineteen
times by cows in the six weeks since we
arrived, and rescued only eleven times from
the depths of the cistern. We have already
invested in chickens. Long legged fowls
stalk to and fro—roosters in full Turkish
costume loiter about the doorstep and
chuckle fiendishly when we appear in re-
mote perspective, waving dish towels to
frighten them away. I don't think I should
be afraid of common poultry—there is nothing blood-curdling in the demure pullet or
the cheerful cock of my youthful recollection—but these singular creatures seem like
wild visions of a disordered mind, the uncanny brood of goblin eggs. With that
beautiful idea of the eternal fitness of things
which characterizes his every action, a certain man has purchased a peacock to adorn
the grounds. This morning I laid a gray
hair significantly across his coat sleeve (the
man's, not the peacock's), merely remark-
ing: "The result, unhappy man, of your evil

voiced bird. Every time he opens his
mouth I think that Gabriel's trump is sounding!"

We had a cow, a guileless, hornless animal with liquid eyes and fragrant breath,
but alas for prophetic custards and golden
cream, she has choked to death with a
turnip!

Our garden; there at least is full fruition
for every promise of delight. This morning
it was a pleasant scene to watch the master
of this fruitful domain march briskly forth
with his shovel and an armful of scrubby
twigs.

"What have you there?" questioned the
"blessed demoizel" from an upper window.

"Crab apples!" came back the blithe re-
sponse.

Perhaps they were, dear, but they looked
like dead switches.

One day I devoted to planting peas.
"How charming," quoth I from the depths
of a yellow sunbonnet, "to invite our city
friends to dine on fresh peas plucked from
our dewy vines!" Next morning broke
over the dreamy world, and discovered those
demon fowls, closely attended by the chant-
ing peacock, scratching my cherished crop

to the surface. I planted them again, this time two feet deep, to circumvent the chickens. "We shall not make ourselves dangerously ill on peas this summer, my dear," was Isaac's brief comment.

Thinking that a country home would be incomplete without a dog, Isaac dragged one home the other night, muzzled and in chains. I might be tempted to approach a bull of Bashan, or trifle with a Bengal tiger, but counted gold would not lure me within ten feet of that brute. He sits upon his haunches in the outhouse and bays bloodily at every foot-fall. He gives us no rest, and the duet of dog and peacock bids fair to quench reason's tremulous spark forever. He will soon die of starvation, as no one dares approach him with food.

But oh! there are lots of lovely things in country living! Such entrancing glimpses of the lake. A pathway of ever-changing opal; an azure heaven fallen earthward like the petal of a violet from its stem; a waste of silver gray flecked with rose and fluted by soft winds! Ah, match me if you can the splendor of my morning walks, by the borders of this inland sea! And the swift miracle of the season's advance! Yester-

day the fields were brown—to-day green as
the sheen of Niagara's plunge; yesterday
the thickets scarce hid the wandering bird;
to-day, though you searched an hour, you
could not find the covert where its shy wing
broods upon its hidden nest. I think after
all, my dear, the pros have it for country
living.

Before we leave our chair and cease our
chatting, let us say a word about walking.
Few women walk gracefully. Few women
know how to walk, and fewer know how to
breathe. The chest does not hold your full
breathing apparatus. The muscles that help
fill the lungs like the handles of the bellows,
lie in the abdomen. Breathe from there;
fill your lungs full, using those poor neglected muscles which tight lacing and ignorance have made almost useless to you. Draw
in breath as you scent a sweet, sweet rose,
with a long, full, deep inhalation; erect your
head, expand your chest; hold yourselves
erect and evenly-poised, without mincing,
or lolling, or bending forward or backward,
and walk away as God meant you should
walk with the graceful stride, and the lis-
some abandon of a young roe. Throw
away French heels, cast off deforming

bustles, fold up your corsets, and be natural. Walk daily in this way, not in the ceaseless round of shopping, but strike for the country roads, where the clover lies in limitless acres of purple bloom, and the turf is as elastic and soft as a velvet pile, and I give you my word, you will daily grow beautiful and be counted with the daughters of the gods!

"What is the matter?" I asked of the big policeman.

"Nothing; only a girl in a fit!" was his answer, as he motioned the crowd back from what seemed to be a struggling bundle of rags thrown down on the rough stones of the alley.

I walked on a few steps, then turned and approached the object about which only men and boys were gathering. A dark, pinched little face, with half-closed eyes and a few flecks of foam about the lips, lay pillowed on a dirty bag full of street refuse. A pair of bony hands, grimed with the soil of contact with all that was noisome and vile, fluttered a little, and were still. Two

eyes that were strangely blue and sweet for
that wan, discolored face stretched wide underneath the smiling of a far-off heaven that
was scarcely more blue than they. A couple
of bare feet laid in a repose that was new
and strange at noonday. A wasted and
shrunken breast, under which the heart of
a more desolate childhood never beat. I
drew as near as I could to the miserable
little creature, then stopped as though a wall
of stone had intervened between us. What
could such delicate creatures as you and I
do with this heap of vermin-infected humanity, my dear? Could we stoop to gather that tangled, dirty little head against the
fresh corsage of our best suit, and bestow
the sacrament of a caressing touch on that
brow which, perhaps, never yet felt the sunshine of love's kiss? Could we sit down
there on the stones and chafe those grimy
hands, or, for decency's sake, throw our own
costly wrap over those distorted limbs?

Why not?

I have no answer, my dear. I can only return, dumbly, glance for glance and agree
with you that we could not afford to do
these things which the Lord of Heaven,
passing by that scene of pain and desolation,

would surely have done. We have not the moral courage to be literal followers of Him whom we sometimes try to serve.

So, with a shudder, I stood aside and watched the indifferent yet not altogether unkindly policemen bear away that mite of wrecked childhood in their arms and carry it lightly to the ambulance. I uttered no word save a half inaudible "poor little thing!"—such as one might have bestowed upon a hurt kitten. I saw the little waif carried away comfortless and desolate to a pauper's bed, and perhaps, by God's good mercy, to a pauper's grave. For what, pray tell me, is a kinder boon for such as she than an early recall from the life that yields them naught but bitterness? Why should we nurse back the flickering flame of vitality in the breast of misery-burdened childhood such as this? Could some great and kindly hand descend from the sky and with discriminating touch separate these sunless, root-blighted weeds from the flowers that fill the King's garden, what a mercy it would be to all! Could all these noisome, pitiful growths be weeded out early and forever, what a solution of humanity's dark problem would be solved! If only bright heads and clean sweet faces were in our way to be caressed and cared for, how much easier we should find it to do our duty and succor the helpless.

But, alas for our delicate sensibilities, our new suits and our perception of what conforms to the proprieties, the hand that weeds the gardens of earth is no discriminating one. It plucks the "wee white rose of all the world" full many a time and spares the nettle and the tare; it will revive to yet more years of misery and squalor and sin this little weed of the streets, and bear away into the "pale realm of death" the idolized and the love-guarded. If we would indeed be doing the Master's work we must stoop, as He did, from the brightness of heaven to the dark depths of hell to find, to succor and to save. Next time we see a beggar dying; next time we see an over-burdened, hard-driven horse; next time we see a cruelly-beaten child; next time injustice or cruelty or want in loathsome shape confronts us, what will we do, I wonder? Just what we have always done, I'll wager a cooky. Pass by on the other side with the white feather of cowardice flaunting in our cap. Afraid of a jest, a sneer, a ribald crowd, when the service that lies within our power to do might bring the peace of heaven into a tortured soul. My dear, I'll give it up. This contradictory human make-up of ours is too much for me. Good-bye.

As I was walking up the avenue the other day, I passed a young and pretty girl, and as she flitted by, I caught the words, "Oh, dear! I wish that I was dead! I shall never, never be happy any more." I wanted to stop and say, "You poor, dear little pocket edition of June, how will you meet the stormy surges further on if the ripples of harbor sailing threaten your soul-craft so disastrously?"

Say as you may, there is an age when we, all of us, find our greatest happiness in being sentimentally wretched. In our teens every shower that falls is a tempest, every disappointment a heart-break. Little butter-lipped school-girls write essays in which life is compared to a "vale of tears," fame to a "bubble," and joy to a "thorny rose." We cultivate "Julia Mills'" friendships, and

drink deeply of the cup of ideal sorrow.
We bear about with us the air of Beard's pictured monkey, sadly questioning of destiny,
"For what was I created?" Nobody understands us; few are congenial, and fewer still
can meet the requirements of our phenome-
nal natures. We are fond of being surprised in tears, and speak of the tomb as of
a welcome resting-place. We like to be con-
sidered delicate, and spend a good deal of
our time writing poetry and reading devo-
tional books. Such epidemics of mental
vaporishness are as natural to youth, sooner
or later, as whooping-cough and measles to
babies, and quite as harmless. When the
genuine sorrows come into our life, they
come, soft-shod. It is the brook that
brawls, not the river. It is the silent snow
that buries up the landmarks, not the fretful
and complaining rain. The sea lashed by
tempest is not so dreaded by mariners as the
windless quiet of becalmed waters. When
we suffer so that our hearts lie like deserts
beneath the vertical glare of heaven, with no
flower of hope to lift its head from the sands
of desolation, and not even the shadow of a
bird's wing of comfort between ourselves
and despair, we are apt to remember the

bread-and-butter days of life with all their little tragedies and burlesque pain, very much as the Amazon might remember the fret of its hillside beginnings, or as bread, baked brown by scorching heat, might remember its days of dough.

The world is very full of desperate trouble, we know. Every heart has its own bitterness to endure as best it may, and yet I will not agree to any doctrine that pronounces life anything but a blessing, and the world anything but a right good place to live in for a while. Life is a beautiful prelude to eternity, like the touch of harps and the sigh of sweet violins that herald the climax of one of Beethoven's symphonies. Did you ever find an April unfollowed by May? No more certain will be the following of sunshine and summer weather after the fitful unrest of the brief space we call life. Only owls and bats seek the shadows and live within them. Only cowards and the faint-hearted call the world a vale of tears. Because there is night-shade in the garden, shall we forego its roses? Because bats live, need we cage them and hang them in our bedrooms? Because it sometimes rains, shall we hoist umbrellas in sunny weather?

Because sin and sorrow, tears and death are abroad in the world, shall we stand constantly at the gate in expectancy of their coming, like children watching for the band to go by, or weep at the windows in neglect of our duties, like old women lingering to see a funeral procession start off?

A day or two ago, a sweet hope perished, or a friend took his place in the festival hall we name heaven, or a child fell asleep in the arms of the death angel, or a flower of love withered upon its frail stalk. Only the Infinite heart knows our sorrow, but behold, while yet the tears fall, the sunshine breaks through them, if but our faith be steady and our courage endures. Somewhere we shall find the hope in blossom, and the friend that left us so suddenly shall hover like a white cloud between us and the sunset gate of death. Somewhere the Death Angel shall lead us up to the child grown into an impossible beauty, and the withered flower we shall find laid within its bosom.

Take heart, then. Do we mourn when hyacinth bulbs break ground, or fruit trees snow the air with tinted blossoms, falling to the earth, that fruit may follow! Death is only the wavering of the blossom, the

bursting of the sheath. Between all vanished joys and friends there swings but a
single gate—one that our last faint dying
breath shall waft ajar. Some day it shall let
us in to where they wait and watch and love
us still. Can we not wait, then, a little while
in patience?

As though to prove the wisdom of my
words, just now, even while I am writing,
the mystic woof of sunshine, shot with rain,
is weaving out of doors. It has been storming like a wild gust of bitter human tears,
but now a rosy tide of sunset floods the drip-
ping world, and the wet streets dimple and
flash like tearful faces smiling. A moment
and the eternal sun wins the victory over
the temporal storm. Away scud the clouds
like beaten gray-coats of old before the advance of our boys in blue. Hurrah for sunshine, then, and banished be the tears!

Fannie is dead. The news came to me in
a letter the other day, and although I ordered no crape, and made no alteration in
the daily procedure of business, yet the

fact that Fannie is dead hangs like a weight at my heart. Fannie was a gentle soul, not without spirit, docile under friendly guidance, restive when unjustly coerced. Her eye was like the depth of a wood-land spring for clearness, and as brown as the under shade of a chestnut. She was the especial friend of those bright years of my life, before a golden hope had dimmed, or a stream run dry. Many a long ramble Fannie and I have had together over meadow roads wet with dew, and up the laural-crowned hills of bright New England. She was not a garrulous companion, indeed if any one ever instanced in her own life the value of golden silence over silver speech, she did. But ah! She was a rare good listener. I never tired of pouring into her ear the confidences I dared not or cared not to impart to those who talked more, yet often knew less. My very first love affair, how well I remember it. The nameless one with whom I gathered the great pound sweets in August (such apples do not grow now a days), the frosted nuts in autumn, and the sweet purple violets in early spring. Why bless your heart, Fannie knew all about that affair long before the folks at home found it out, and I think it was her somewhat reserved bearing when we talked the matter over; a certain disapproval in those gentle eyes into whose liquid depths alas! I shall never look again, that decided me not to chance the irrevocable throw on love's first dream. If restless youth found no worse counsel than you were wont to give dear Fan, I think the wrecks would be fewer along the shores of life. No thought of unworthy speech, or corrupt advice arises to-night to sully the memory of our faithful friendship. No remembered disloyalty casts a shadow athwart the years. No black wine of a recalled ingratitude settles like dregs in the cup I quaff to the memory of faithful Fan.

Beyond a certain friskiness of disposition that led her occasionally into trouble, and a madcap tendency at times to take a five barred gate at a bound, or caper around the garden like a mad thing, scaring steady going old ladies and little children not a little, Fannie was absolutely perfect. How well I remember the old red home where she lived. It was gable roofed and almost windowless, built midway between a clover pasture and a belt of birchen wood. Here she dwelt alone, and yet she was never lonely,

for the corridors of the quaint old house
were always echoing with children's voices.
There was a certain perfume of which Fannie was very fond, and I never catch the
scent of new mown hay, but I recall the
pleasant chamber where she rested when at
home. It was there that Frank, my preach-
er cousin Frank, the boy who went out to
India long ago to become a bald-headed,
fat old missionary, first surprised us with
his ministerial gifts. I owe him a grudge for
those hours of torment in which he preached
"hell-fire" to me until my young flesh turned
purple with terror, and Fannie from her
fragrant corner, uttered often an exclama-
tion of impatient protest; Sam Jones in his
loftiest brimstone flights, never soared higher than Frank used to, perched on the cover
of an old meal chest, with poor little tow-
headed me, for his one hardened and unre-
generate hearer. In that well ventilated
home, through which a draught was always
blowing sometimes laden with the fragrance of fruit trees all in bloom, sometimes
with the damp, sweet odor of the wood,
sometimes with honey from the billows of
sweet grasses falling like foam in the wake
of the mower's scythe, the little golden
17

headed baby played, the little sister whose dimpled feet grew tired so early, and turned aside to rest forever.

Ah, to-night I see again those little fingers wreathed in Fannie's chestnut hair, and hear the prattle of those laughing lips as she talked her baby talk to ever listening Fannie! One night, when we were all asleep in the great house, our father was awakened by an unwonted noise, and listening, hardly half awake, he turned to the sleepy mother, saying:

"Why, that is Fannie, under the window! What can she want here this time of night!" And rising he found our house in flames, and knew that but for faithful Fannie's alarm, we all might have miserably perished together. So after that we grew to regard Fannie, not only as our friend, but as our preserver. And father said:

"The gable-roofed house where she has lived from her birth, shall be her home until her death, and boys, I charge you, if I die and Fanny grows old and of little service, as the old are apt to be, that you make her last days happy and full of plenty." So Fannie has lived in the old homestead ever since. Not a hair of her chestnut locks

turned gray; hardly a muscle of her proud
strength relaxed. To be sure the madcap
spirit of her youth toned down to decorous
reserve, and the flash in her brown eye took
on a paler light, as a taper will when burning in the dawn-lit house, but Fannie never
grew to be a dullard with advancing years.
They tell me she died at last, as quietly as a
child falls into slumber after hearty play.
And I am right glad to know it, and I am
still more glad to think that in some special
part of the Heaven where we are going, a
corner fenced off from the singing folk and
the harpers, I may, perhaps, find old Fannie waiting to welcome me; her slender
nose pointing through the bars as of yore;
her lithe ears advanced; her big eyes full of
joy at my coming, as in the good old days
on the homestead farm she used to stand to
meet me at the pasture bars—my dear old
horse; my trusty Fan!

If I were asked to-night which of many
gifts I should desire for the little child I love
best in all the world, I should answer, a
contented spirit. Not the mere animal con-

tentment that makes a man satisfied with any condition in life, as the swine with its wallow, but that higher spirit that leads a child of the Heavenly King to hold himself as well content with any dispensation of his Father's will. Look about you a little now and then, and mark how few of us have really great trials to bear. There are millions of poor people in the world, and to be very poor is no doubt to miss many of the good things of this life. But to suffer the deprivations of luxury and miss the warmth of the purple robe, is, after all, a matter that need only touch the perishable part of us. If we pray constantly to be delivered from the sordidness of poverty, we will find that even poverty may be borne. If we serve what little we may have in a well-ordered and cleanly way, the little will be more apt to prove sufficient for our needs. I once visited a home where the bread-winner was a widow. There were lots of growing children to be cared for, and the income was worn threadbare in the passing. But at every meal there was pleasant talk and loving counsel, the linen and the jests were of equal cleanliness, and the merry-making of the boys seemed to vie in purity with the

sparkle of the paltry show of glass-ware, so
that I think there have been courtly spreads
of less cheer than that of the little table in
the poor woman's humble home. Some
way poverty lost its sting in that love-
sunned circle. I knew that grinding care
gnawed often at the mother's weary heart,
and that the long nights frequently found
her patching and darning the ragged scraps
of clothes until day was almost ready to
knock at the gates of dawn, but it was only
the surface of things that was ever shadowed
by the dark wing of want. The inner depths
of that woman's soul lay ever like a lake that
reflects the blue of heaven. When I used to
sit and watch her, I longed for the gift of
dear old Titbottom's spectacles, that I might
look beyond the pale, pinched body, and behold the verity of her sweet and contented
soul.

I think I should have found her similitude
in the vision of a mountain-brook, which,
through devious ways, and over sharp and
ragged stones, sings ever of the glorious sea
to which it hastens, and is fed from the hills
from whence cometh more than mortal help.

To be poor need not mean to be abject;
nor need it mean to be pinched and starved

in spirit. The Son of the King has royal blood in his veins, and its needs must show itself; in sharing his little with those that have less; in gentle courtesies and tender forbearances. How is any poverty going to affect the soul, if a man is born with that sort of royal blood in his veins? Don't think that I mean to say that a man with an inadequate income, or a poor woman with a back-load of drudgeries, is going to preserve perpetual affability and eternal sweetness of spirit.

Was there ever a summer that did not carry a sheath of dark days in its bosom? Who would appreciate June if there were no March? Poverty will fling a shadow over the soul, and render many homes so dark and gruesome, that it is as impossible for that soul to blossom out into amiable speeches and sunny actions, as for a rose to unfold its petals out of time, but, thank God, we judge of summer by the average, not by the special spells of weather. If at the end we can speak of gathered flowers and garnered harvests, we know that the season, on the whole, has been a success, no matter how many rainy, grumbly days there may have been. Did you ever thank

God for that little clause, "as much as is possible?" He knew quite well it was impossible to live forever at peace with men and circumstances. Can a bird sing all the time? It is to our credit, my dear, if we foot up a fair average of sunshine and song by and by when the season is over and ended. So I say that it is not in the power of poverty to blast a life that carries the royal blood in its veins. If you are a child of heaven, you cannot keep the heritage of heaven out of your heart, any more than the year can forego its four weeks of June. It is not in the power of old clothes and scrimpy food, and low ceilings to render you forgetful of the many mansions that are awaiting you, and the "white robes" and the sparkling crown, when these few brief years of life in an alien land are forgotten.

Only keep your thoughts on what is coming, and the discomforts of earthly deprivation and want will pass over you as shadows pass over the depths of the sea, or darkness settles upon a garden full of fragrant-hearted roses.

But some of us have other and greater trials than poverty brings. We are sick, and the members that God intended to be like

the strong chords of a perfect harp, are all
untuned by the hand of pain, so that life is
only a jangle. of discordant notes instead of
a serene and joyful psalm. That is hard to
bear. No harder lot was ever laid on man
since Eden cast its first white blossom at
the feet of Israel. But stop and think about
it a minute. To be sure you are "shut in,"
but what does it mean to be shut in? It
means to be folded like a sick lamb out of
the cold and the winter storm. It means to
be hid in a pavilion where no flying arrow
can pierce your heart, and no sharp-shoot-
ing temptation can lay you low. Your days
are spent within a cloister where dark-robed
pain presides, but where the air is full of
prayerful peace rather than of stinging care
and bristling wrong doing. The Lord has
been very good to you in that He has kept
you away from those defilements which
might have trailed the white fabric of your
soul in the dust of evil desire and weakly
yielded wrong. This pain has been your
savior. Without it who knows how far you
might have wandered from the bosom of
God wherein you now lie like a little child.
And no earthly suffering can endure very
long. It may seem an endless time now,

but looking back from the golden uplands
of heaven, what a very little gap among the
eternal hills this "valley of tears" shall make.
Believe me, the longest life of pain shall
seem of small consequence, when "Christ
Himself shall stoop at last to gather your
life's rose, and smile away your mortal to
divine." The tenderest angel sent to draw
our earth-born thoughts toward heaven may
wear the badge of pain, and looking back
upon our lot at last, it may be very easy to
say, "It was the best."

Are you tormented by faithless friends,
and broken constancies? Does it seem to
you that nobody in all the world had so
much to bear from the smiting hand of injustice and the carking tooth of ingratitude?

A traveler passing through a foreign
country puts up at a wayside inn. The beds
are hard, the service poor, the fees exor-
bitant, but he carries in his bosom a letter
that bids him press on, and come home.
Does he sorrow much over the discomforts
of the inn or the cupidity of its retainers?
Why! bless your heart, to-morrow he is going home, and everything will be straight-
ened out there.

Were your worst betrayals of trust ever

so bad as those that befell a better than you, when even Peter denied Him? Could the accumulated injustice of the world match the single injustice of Pilate's charge? Was desertion so absolute ever meted to a human soul as that garden's lonely watcher knew when even God seemed to have gone away and left the pitying heavens untenanted? And yet you and I cover our faces with our hands and mourn the pitiful betrayals and injustices of our lot, while we have it in our power to count this risen King over every possible sorrow our friend? Having tasted the sting of every sorrow, and sounded the plummet of ingratitude and despair, He stands over against each revelation of human grief with divine healing in His hands for all our bruises and all our wounds.

There is nothing, then, not poverty nor want, nor pain nor grief, nor death itself, that can keep us out of the heritage of sure-coming joy if we bear in our bosom the jewel of a contented mind, and in our soul an unwavering trust in the tenderness of the All-Loving One.

CHAPTER VI.

I read once in a quaint little book, of a man whose life was embittered by the heritage of a curious pair of spectacles left him by his grandfather. Through them, he was forced to view the world and the people within it, as they in reality were, and not as they seemed. All shams resolved themselves into original nothingness before him, and the great tanglement of life unwound itself in every gleam of his wonderful glasses.

The poor old fellow didn't have a very blissful time of it, and I think when the great day dawned that carried him and his spectacles out of the world, he was glad to go. But I should like to borrow his glasses a little while for all that. So many things get mixed up here, like a gardener's collection of seeds with the labels all wrong; here a package of garden pinks labeled wild onions, or a bunch of carrots marked "lily bulbs."

Sitting in my office window to-day, with people flocking by, like sea gulls before a

storm, what strange sights I could see had I
but old Titbottom's spectacles astride my
nose. Here comes a woman with a face like
a Madonna. "How sweet," "how pure,"
"how faultless," cries the world. I look, and
lo; a shaft of ice, a slab of stone, a marble
heart.

Here comes another whom the world calls
trifling, giddy, without earnest purpose or
steady aim. I look, and see a singing fountain sparkling in the sun, a rivulet of mountain water, making the earth green with
its own ministration of joy. Here comes
a correct specimen of what all the world
holds to be above reproach. Her eyelids
droop over eyes that are like hooded nuns
ever at prayer, so devout and concentrated
their glances. Her character is a white
cloak which the idle fingers of gossip have
never sought to hold aside. I look, and lo;
a Magdalen unrepentant. A snake lies
curled amid the withered lilies of her heart.
Here comes a poorly dressed, shabby girl.
Surely her beauty has blighted the whiteness of its own innocence, as the canker may
eat the heart of the rose that nourishes it.
You fling an idle word of scorn as she goes
by, and have no doubt but that she is hardly

worth your pity. I look, and behold; a snow-
flake settling down through leaden skies,
born of Heaven. Those men, clean-palmed
and of faultless attire, whom mothers
court for their innocent daughters, and with
whose names Dame Grundy heads her list
of irreproachables; my glasses show them
to be rude swine; or fruit dead and decayed
at core. The pompous man, swelling like
a spring freshet with his own importance,
is but a crackling bit of paper, marked with
higher or lower bank value. I see wives
clinging to and surrounding with beautiful
devotion, mere pork tubs and money tills.
I see husbands cherishing in their bosoms,
bits of rumpled lace, or soiled fabrics, or artificial flowers. And then, perhaps, old lady,
I turn the glasses on myself, and what I see
makes me more charitable towards others,
more loving, and less critical.

As long as Titbottom took his spectacles
with him when he died, and remembering
that their possession only embittered his
heart and made a cynic of him, let us try,
good people, to substitute for them a charity which shall seek to cover rather than ex-
pose the faults and counterfeits of our neighbors. All the tears and deplorements in

the world won't turn a field of Canada thistles into a rose garden. But a flower seed, dropped wherever we can, may make an oasis now and then to brighten up the wilderness.

I have just a word to say to-day about what big fellows owe to "little ones"—of what fair play means and how to keep the heaven-lighted fire of chivalry aglow in the breast. Ridicule is the coward's weapon. The big boy who will throw stones at a rabbit is a good prototype of the man or the woman who ridicules the peculiarities or the physical defects of a fellow creature. You owe tenderness and the loan of the mantle of concealment to anyone with whom you may be thrown whose eccentricities or personal blemishes may make him or her the object of curious regard.

* * * * *

The unrepressed smile or the whipcord word may stab deeper than any knife, and

make a wound that will bleed forever.
Young girls are the sweetest things in the
world outside the realm of birds and blossoms, and yet they often do the cruelest
things. Why, my dear, your very beauty
and winsomeness oblige you to be consid-
erate of those whom nature has made less
fair and sweet. "Noblesse oblige" is not
more binding than this law that compels you
to be tenderly thoughtful of these "little
ones" whom you constantly hurt. A
thoughtless school girl is often more cruel
than the Cæsars, and a rollicky school boy
out-Neros Nero in his reckless disregard of
a schoolmate's sensibilities.

* * * * *

Give a stupid person the benefit of a
doubt. We cannot all roar like lions, and
yet in the great orchestra of nature the katy-
did has its place as well as the king of
beasts. Because some "little ones" sit gog-
gle-eyed and silent in the midst of such fine
roaring, do not doubt but what, when their
opportunity comes, they can chirp like good
fellows. Give them a chance, I say, and

even then, if they won't take it, don't call them uninteresting and stupid. Katydids were not meant to sing by lamplight and in crowds. When the noise lulls and the lights are out their disputations begin, and last when sweeter singers are locked in slumber. In company, then, don't place all the silent people with fools; yield them the deference due to those who merely wait their opportunity.

* * * * *

Bashful people are claimants for chivalry. When you can quietly step to the rescue of a bashful person do so. Perhaps you will know some day what a sunburst of blessings went from that rescued heart in your behalf. And, I can tell you, no smallest deed of service ever went unblessed, any more than the sun shines in April without creating a blossom.

* * * * *

Avoid unkind criticism. If a life be pure, let all its little oddities alone. If you are convinced that some not over-bright young man is trying to live a clean life in the world and make an honest record, don't pick him to pieces, girls, in your after-party talks. A pure man is sometimes better than a clever man, and truth and honor make a better showing than wit.

* * * * *

Make your aim in the world to leave happy hearts in your wake, as the woman spoken of in the play of "Clio" made the "grain a little greener for her footfall passing by." Strive not so much to be admired as to be loved, and seek that love in shy places among the little ones of earth.

The other morning I was standing in front of a looking-glass. It was a matter of necessity rather than of pleasure, and as I sought to tie the bow of my collar-ribbon I gazed with something of contempt at my own reflection. But while I gazed, a mysterious feeling of terror took possession of me, so that, if I had not turned away, I think I should have gone mad. Whence came the phantom that looked into my eye from the depth of that mirror? Whither was it going? What was it? How long would it tarry? It was all that I should ever know of the personality that signs my autograph, loves my friends and despises my enemies. If I had a million dollars to pay for the chance, I could never come any nearer than this to looking into the eyes that window the perplexing Ego that is my soul. I might gaze forever into the depths of these reflected orbs, but what are they? Shadows born of the union of quicksilver and crystal, which a blow would shatter. This moment the something called "I" stands here and confronts me, but where will it be to-morrow, next year, or when eternity, never begun and forever unending, is a billion ages on its course? Before this present day's completed span is run, it may exist no longer in all the spaces of the sentient earth; within a week it may be laid away under the parched turf; as the years drift by it shall be as completely forgotten as the petals of Sappho's rose. Meantime where will this inexplicable phantom which confronts me from those eyes in the looking-glass be gone? They can never bury it, however deep they dig its grave. Will it slip away, like a ray of light, to mirror itself, perhaps, within the translucent tide of eternal life, or lose itself with other sun-sparkles in the fine radiance of illimitable ether.

Once upon a time it came to pass that there wandered through a great city a woman who was wasted and worn with the carrying of many bundles.

And the rain beat upon that woman so that she tottered like another Lear, the sport of scornful elements.

And the umbrella, which a too previous friend had palmed off upon her, flapped to and fro in the wind like a sail which no wind filleth.

And by reason of its unmanageableness it came to pass that the passage of the woman through the crowded streets was a menace to those that walked before and after her.

And many lifted up the voice in protest, crying: "Verily it cannot be that a woman carrieth an umbrella so but what she gougeth out the eyes and lifteth on high the hat-brim of the sons of men that walk to and fro upon the highways."

And it came to pass that the woman, being possessed of a spirit of wrath by reason of the umbrella, and likewise of many draperies and countless bundles, cast the umbrella from her and strode forward unprotected beneath the down-pouring heavens.

Now a certain cabman (one who drove a vehicle called a hansom), being idle, and like a beast of prey seeking one whom he might devour, accosted the woman, saying but one word, namely, "cab?"

And the one word he uttered was unaccompanied by any sign whereby the woman might have taken alarm unto herself and so escaped the destiny that awaited her.

Now, the woman being worn and wasted, and stricken with sudden years, so that she would have fallen, replied unto the man, saying, "Yea, verily."

And she entered the cab, she and the bundles fate had cast upon her.

Then the cab horse, being possessed of many demons, stood upon its hind legs and smote the air with joy that he and his master had found a victim.

And it came to pass that the passage of that cab through the streets was like the way a hose-cart cleaveth when the alarm of fire is in the air, or like the track of a ball that flyeth from a prize pitcher's hand, or like the flight of a strong eagle to the sun.

And the woman was cast to and fro upon the seat like a pea in a wind-shaken pod.

And she cried aloud, but in the tumult of her advance her voice was like the wailing of a sorrowful babe.

And suddenly the horse fell, and the woman was cast forth upon the watery pavement, she and the wrecked bundles she bore with her.

And the cabman, being but little hurt, assisted his horse to its feet, and would have replaced his victim in her seat.

But, being gifted with the gift of ready speech, the woman confronted him, saying:

"Behold, I have vowed many vows and uttered unto myself many resolves, yet when my memory slept I have forgotten those vows and entered thy cab.

"Now hear me while I say that though the heavens pour boiling water, and the pavements run flaming fire, I, nor the generation of my name that come after me, nor the handmaid who reigneth in my kitchen, nor the dog who devastateth the wardrobe of my children—nay, not even the stranger who asketh my command, shall ride from thenceforth even forever within thy terrible cabs.

"Go to, thou man of guile; thou and the horse that Satan furnished thee.

"I will die, the good Lord willing, in my bed, when the fullness of my time draweth nigh, but thou and thy two-wheeled trap of death shall know me no more forever."

And the man of the cab went his way, drawn mightily by the horse possessed of many demons.

And the woman likewise went her way, still grasping to her aching breast her many bundles.

And it came to pass that the ways of the cabman and of the woman lay far apart from that time forth forever, and will never again be the same as long as the woman knoweth herself.

If there is a quality in this world, whicn, like material gold is bound to be counter-feited, and its spurious imitation palmed off for the genuine, it is enthusiasm. What the breeze is to sultry summer weather, or what

sunshine is to the growing world, such is
enthusiasm to any nature. Like the fiz of
a bottle of poor beer or the combustion of
a wet fire-cracker, such is all mere gush.
The crackling of thorns under a pot, or the
twitter of tomtits, is not more senseless.
Many good people are afraid to express the
half of what they feel, for fear of being
ranked with the gusher. Never fear! The
difference between the spurious and the
true is easily detected. Speech takes unto
itself the happy medium of glowing eyes and
flushed cheeks when the heart is really
moved. But when the emotion is only as-
sumed, speech mounts stilts and is apt to
tumble.

Shall we briefly photograph the gushing
girl of to-day? She usually cultivates simplicity, and an æsthetic style. Blue is her
favorite color, and she affects white muslin
and rosebuds. A child-like smile completes
her make-up.

Brown, a rising journalist, is often in her
company, and to him she breathes an appreciation of his Swinburnesh verse that is rapture to the young man's soul. "Ah, dear,
dear, friend," she will say to him, "there
was that in your poem to-day that breathed

over my soul like a strong wind out of paradise. How can I thank you? Sometimes I fear," here she struggles with a blush, "that such a mere babe as I, in worldly knowledge—" here young Periwinkle saunters by and casually observes:

"Fine sunset to-night. Did you notice it, Miss Glint?"

"Oh, indeed, yes," she warbles; "was it not just heavenly? Such sweet tints, and ravishing distances! Oh, Mr. Periwinkle, I often long, when looking upon such delicious sunsets"—here the hostess interrupts:

"Miss Glint, will you sing for us?"

"Please excuse me. Save to warble a few wild notes at eventide for pa, I never sing. But if you insist, I will do my tiny, unpretending best!"

So she carols snatches of "Love's Young Dream," with emotion and perverted accent.

As a fellow traveler the gushing girl is worse than mosquitoes. She stands before Niagara with a simpering shout of—"Ain't it lovely?"

She greets Yosemite with, "Ain't it sweet?" She is boosted up Mount Blanc, and gasps, "Ain't it splendid?" She sits down to a supper of hot flap-jacks, and cries, "Ain't they magnificent!" A mountain, a waterfall, and a pancake, alike, arouse her rapture. A mouse will throw her into convulsions, so will a rattlesnake, so would Gabriel's trumpet. She keeps a diary, wherein she rhapsodizes and gurgles like a dying hen. Take a sample extract:

"Visited Rosehill, to-day. Wore my violet suit. Oh, the sad sorrow of this suggestive spot! Soon shall I rest beneath these daisies! Oh, W. M., shall we understand each other's intense, but dumb forbearance, in the Heaven land!" (Tear drops and dashes!) An unfailing characteristic of the gushing girl is her assurance that nobody understands her.

She walks through life in a Sahara of her own making. She often sends poems to the flint-hearted editors, scattered through the land, and when they return them with a nice little printed apology for so doing, she weeps, but does not wonder. How could a horrid man have sympathy with the Æolian qualities of her transcendental soul!

As she advances in years she grows worse. We can bear with gushing in a girl, but there should be a special clause inserted in the litany—"Good Lord, deliver us from gushing old women."   At forty-nine we find her rampant in the field of the Woman Suffragist Crusade.   She is shrill and denunciatory in her comments upon the "horrid men," and trips airily down the warpath that leads to his total extermination.   Did you not read, the other day, an extract from her speech in Washington, "I feel like a dove ready for battle!   A starbeam in the arena of bloodshed!"

Thus in the ever increasing tide of disappointed, crabbed and foolish women, the gushing girl is swept away.   She appears at the surface now and then, voluble, frantic; but nobody listens.   And so, farewell thou tropic-souled and trippy tongued sister!   R. I. P.

But I pray you, good people, take heed, lest you mar the beauty of your enjoyment of life, by confounding this gush with heartfelt enthusiasm.   Enthusiasm, in any nature, is the dew that keeps alive the heart's freshness and bloom.   To unnecessarily restrain it, is like stripping the blossoms off the trees and leaving nothing but firm little balls of immature fruit.

The rosy petals of the blossom are all

prodigal; there is no utility to them—but where would the flush be on May's fair cheek, or the coronet on June's bright brow, without them?

Neither imagine, because you are growing old, that you must fold away the quick appreciations and impulses of youth with your own youthful garments. Don't think, because you are a man of business, or a sedate matron, that enthusiasm is out of character. There never was a forest so dark, or an autumn so late, that the sunshine could not filter through and change the gloom to vague, sweet twilight. There should never be a heart grow too worldly or too old, to forget to worship beauty and loveliness wherever found, whether in the evanescent bloom of sunset cloud, or in the spirit charm of a perfect character.

I am inclined to think that I envy "Little Tommy Tucker" above all other heroes of juvenile lore. What a splendid time Tom had! No bars of conventional restraint to keep him out of the clover. No Prince Albert coats and society manners. No tight boots, high collars, or soft corns. If Tom took it into his happy-go-lucky head to travel, away he went with nobody nigh to hinder. He never had to bother about baggage checks, lower berths and porters' fees. His trunk never went astray, his shirt-bosoms were never squeezed in the packing, his toothbrush never was left behind and his robe de nuit never got covered with shoe blacking. All he had to do when he became hungry was to take a troche and go out and sing a song in the twilight until some tender heart came along and provided him with a supper fit for the young gods. For tell me, please, if any menu prepared by a French chef and served in seventeen courses ever matched the good, sweet bread and butter of our childhood's days. Terrapin is good, and the oysters washed down with plenty of champagne is good, ices and creams and all sorts of savory confections are good, but with one and all troop those handmaids of death—apoplexy, gout, acute dyspepsia and a softened brain. It is not by disasters of wind, or wreck, or tide that men flock fastest to the doom of the grave, but simple overeating carries them thither at the rate of 10,000 a day. Lightning strikes

one man where hot pastry and spiced meat
kills twenty. I would rather take my chance
at another Gettysburg than come in daily
range of a mince pie.

* * * * *

So, Tommy Tucker, my boy, I would like
nothing better than to join you in your
vagabond career this very day. For I am
sick of well-behaved Jack Horners and
their plums of plenty; I am sick of fuss and
tired of feathers. I long to be a sun-
bonneted woman and live on the edge of a
prairie, where I can hear the meadow-larks
sing. I want to forget the clang of cables
and rejoice in the whippoorwill's lament and
the cricket's din instead. I want to be a
cowboy and tent on a thousand-acre ranch.
I want to become utterly oblivious to that
part of life devoted to money-getting and
become a sublimated being who shall know
no excitement greater than driving home
the cows and hunting hens' nests; no dissi-
pations deeper than drinking buttermilk,
and no diet richer than old-fashioned bread
and butter, served in a clean kitchen off a
deal table that is whiter than snow. When
I shall come to that estate of primitive and

healthful simplicity, perhaps I shall find you, Tom, bare-footed and homespun clad, waiting to join hands in a race for the supper, earned without a heartache and paid for with a song.

There is another character in Mother Goose lore which is almost as great a favorite with me as young Tucker. In old Mother Hubbard my heart has always found delight, first for her directness and next for her exclusiveness. Roundabout people are tiresome. They are like carpenters who spend all day in driving one shingle-nail. A direct stroke hits the nail on the head at once. Did you ever see a hen cross a garden? Is there a flake of dirt within six feet of her track which she does not scratch for the worm that isn't there? Ten to one it is right under her nose, while she travels all around Robin Hood's barn to get it. Did you ever see our neighbor's wife try to get out of the room after she has said good-night and it was time for her to go? She keeps her asthmatic husband in a draught fully ten minutes, and forces you to remain standing as long, although your back aches and your feet burn like hot biscuit from a hard day's work, all because she hasn't Mother Hubbard's splendid gift of directness and straight-about-edness. Once having made up their mind to do a thing, I love to see people do it. When the old dame started for her cupboard she went! She didn't go half way and then turn back to say a last word. She didn't take in the library or loiter in the music-room. She thought cupboard, and she accomplished cupboard. She might have said to herself, "I really must look into that cupboard some time to-day," and then sat down with a novel, or practiced over a new piece, and forgotten all about it, to the detriment of a too confiding dog.

* * * * *

I know a girl, and I am willing to bet a cooky that you know another, who will form a fine set of resolutions for the conduct of the day and never carry one of them out. For instance she will say, "Now if I live I will face the skirt of my worn dress this very hour;" or, "I will surely write that letter to-day;" or, "providence permitting, I will not go to sleep to-night until I have sewed on my dear father's coat button." She means well, but through lack of that

straightforward directness that character-
ized Old Mother Hubbard she allows herself to be side-tracked by some trivial circumstance, and her resolutions come to
naught. Let me say one thing to you, girls,
and remember I love you all the time I am
saying it; after you have made up your
mind to do a thing, go ahead and do it,
though temptation to take another track beset you behind and before. Let it be said of
you "she went!" rather than "she tarried!"
After the duty is accomplished, then read
your record and sing your song.

* * * * *

Another trait I admire in Mother Hubbard as portrayed in the nursery jingle is
her exclusiveness. She kept something
locked up. It was only a bone, but she kept
it in a closet. She didn't lay it out on the
kitchen table to advertise her poverty. She
had the delicacy to keep her affairs to herself. Had she wrapped her bone in a paper
and laid it in a corner ten to one the neighbors would have hauled her over the coals
for untidy ways. Bones draw mice, even
when kept in cupboards, but mice under
lock and key are not so trying to the nerves

and don't scatter so much rubbish as mice
that roam at large. To be sure the poor old
lady didn't find the bone when she got there,
but that wasn't her fault. She had put it
there, and had perfect faith that she should
find it when with promptness and dispatch
she went to her cupboard. Learn of the
grand old dame to keep something set apart,
hidden, as it were, from busybodies and gossips. It is all very delightful to be frank and
free, to bear the reputation of being hail-
fellow well met with everybody who comes
along. But there is such a thing as cheap-
ening ourselves by our laxity of tongue and
manners. The good book says, "Love thy
neighbor as thyself," but it doesn't say, "Tell
thy neighbor all that thou knowest." Of
the two, perhaps the overconfiding fellow
is the best comrade, but the fellow who
knows enough to keep an occasional bone
in the closet leaves the best record behind
him, when the glamor of an evanescent wit
and the fascination of a garrulous tongue
are forgotten. This is an age of excessive
and rampant equality.

There is a hodge-podge about things in
general that reminds one of Pennsylvania
scrapple—everything under the sun mingled

19

in one batch of dough and baked in one
dish. There are some of us who don't like
it. We do not relish contiguities that are
quite so close and a shoulder to shoulder
march with the commonplace and the alike.
One thing remains for us to do—keep some
of our bones under lock and key. Let us be
able to say to ourselves, "Here is this great
table d'hote served on the co-operation plan.
Here I must sit and nibble crusts with Tom,
Dick and Harry, whether I like or not, but
thank goodness there is a bone in my cupboard for me and my dog alone. I would
rather pick it by myself, with faithful Tray
for company, than eat planked shad in public with the greedy masses."

* * * * *

There is one more heroine of Mother
Goose fiction to which I would call your attention. Her name is unchronicled, but her
type is multiform. To classify her under a
personal nomenclature would be like calling
the grasshopper by name out of a Kansas
wheatfield. All that the rhyme records of
her is an unappeasable appetite and an un-
conquerable restlessness. She fed upon
everything that comes within the broad

scope of "victuals and drink" and yet "could
never keep quiet." When I see large women
with flabby chins and infinite abdominal
girth I know that they are no relation by
either blood or brain to the restless one of
my theme. She was thin and nothing that
she ate went to flesh. She might have consumed custard by the ton and cream by the
gallon, yet would she have been the slender-
est blade of mortality that ever flashed from
its scabbard. She had large haunting eyes,
and they were full of somber gleam, like a
lake overbrooded by a cloud-swept moon.
She had a something within her that beat
her frail body as an untamed eagle beats its
bars, and do you suppose "goodies" ever yet
satisfied eagles when they wanted to fly?
There is a divinely given restlessness that
proves our breed—thank God if you have it,
although it may be uncomfortable. The
turkey strutting in the barnyard, and ap-
peasing every aspiration with corn, is a
vastly more enjoyable bird, both alive and
in the pot, than the eagle that soars, and
screams, and defies the lightning from his
storm-rocked eyrie, but the full culmination
of all life is not to be found in the dinner-
pot, nor scratched out of a compost heap.

I would rather be the unquiet, brainy little woman, whom "goodies" failed to soothe, even if I went down to my grave torn and ragged with life's inadequacy, than be the fat, sleepy, easy-going woman I meet from day to day in restaurants, upon whom a chicken fry acts like one of King David's psalms and whose capacity is bounded by victuals and drink.

Get up and smite the cymbals, then, if you are lean and hollow-eyed and sullen; it is a sign that you are going to be filled out some day with something better than beans and beer and more soothing than cake and flummery.

The fire had burned down to a handful of smoldering embers, weird shadows flickered now and then across the rude walls, and without, an icy rain was falling drearily. Now and then a shrill blast, like the cry of some one in distress sounded through the streets and died away in hoarse and fitful sobbings. Within the room sat one who was bent with toil, and old before her time with care. The scanty locks drawn tightly back disclosed a brow that was lined with deep furrows, and underneath, in their cavernous sockets, burned ruthlessly a pair of dark, bright eyes.

About her shoulders was drawn the remnant of a faded shawl, and now and then a rattling cough shook her slight form convulsively. She was steadily working at a pile of unfinished shirts that lay like snow drifts all about the dreary room. Her hands shook like those of a paralytic, and interposed betweeen the lamp, they would scarcely more hinder the passage of the light, than a withered rose. Suddenly she dropped her work and her head fell forward in what seemed an irresistible stupor of sleep. Then it was that there came a strange and clanking tread up the outer stair, like the jar of many wheels, and the slight door shook as a heavy body fell against it.

"Who is it?" cried the woman, starting from her sleep.

"The sewing woman's enemy! Open to the spirit of the sewing machine," came the answer, like the click of a rattling shuttle.

"But I did not know you for an enemy. I thought the sewing machine was our friend and abettor rather than our foe," replied the woman as she undid the door and gave entrance to a strange figure, with a head like a revolving wheel and the feet of a dancing treadle. Tramp, click, roll, over the floor came the object, and flinging aside the pile of shirts, as a snow shovel attacks a drift, it settled itself noisily by the woman's chair.

"Yes," it said whirrily, "behold in me the friend that has baffled your efforts to make a living; that has devoured your freshness and your bloom, as the dragon once devoured the flower of maidenhood and devastated the land. I am the stomachless worker that needs not rest. I am the worker wrought of steel and without sensibilities or nerves; that needs no recreation. Because I can do five times your work with no sort of keep or hire. I have usurped your needle and the dainty craft that once made your skill desirable. When manufacturers can make with me a dozen shirts with only one pair of tired feet to set me flying, and one pair of dim and heavy eyes like yours to keep me straight, in the time it took you to make one, think you they can keep up your prices or give you anything like a profit on your work?"

"I never thought of it before," said the woman, "but now I see you speak the truth. But what can be done to remedy it all? Can nothing re-instate the old methods, and give us proper pay again for our hard and wearisome work? Look at this coarse shirt;" holding up a workman's woolen garment, as she spoke; "for the making of this I get eight cents, and for a finer one never more than twenty."

"Nothing can be done to retard the march of progress," answered the Sewing Machine, and as he spoke, his belt-band broke with suppressed emotion; "this is an age of advancement, of patents, of scientific development; and we cannot stay the onward sweep of the world's growth. The harvester suffers with you, from the machine that takes the toil of twenty men, and leaves nineteen idle in the field; the trades of every kind are finding machines to do man's work, and of course with ten thousand hands left idle, it is hard to find work for them to do. It took a dozen men a week once, with cradle and scythe, and rake to clean up a harvest field; and those men were always at work and never thought of strikes or shortened hours. Now a combination machine tears through a field and does the twelve men's work in an afternoon. The men made idle, grow restless, and ferment disturbance, as cider standing still makes vinegar. But I have stayed too long. The hour strikes that calls back our spirits to the materialism that we serve. But before I go, one word. Let women tone down their frantic zest for bargains; put less work on a dollar nightgown, and let some of the profit go to the toiling hands that tucked and trimmed and ruffled it, as well as to the merchant who sells it, and you will not be so pinched and worn and ground to a keen edge by poverty. While competition runs a neck-to-neck race with avaricious greedy buyers there is not much left to keep the sewing woman from starving!"

A rumble, a grumble, and a roll, and the poor woman rubbed her sleepy eyes. She was alone!

We all of us know that the solution to the great domestic-service problem lies through the straight road of simplification. When we retrench our requirements according to the limit of our simplest needs we shall

begin to see a solution to much that per-
plexes us in the present aspect of things.
Abolish the dozen superfluous dishes and
depend upon the essential one, and one part
of domestic service is lightened 50 per cent.
It is a half day's work to wash the dishes
after a pretentious modern dinner. Too
many courses, too many fancy pieces, too
much style has made of what should be an
offhand chore, an ordeal of skilled labor.
Thanksgiving dinner used to taste better in
the old days when everything was served in
one course and there was no dainty bread
and butter bric-a-brac, bone plates and individual pieces for everything served, than
it does now when too much style hampers
the fun and crazes the serving woman.
Throw out the nonessentials everywhere
and retain only essentials. Lighten the
work and make household duties what they
ought to be, an easy task rather than an
unending drudgery.

I do not mean to be understood even as
saying that pretty things are nonessentials.
The more attractive you make life the
easier it runs, but prettiness and preten-
sion are two different things. I can make
my table as pretty with a bunch of clover

in a 50-cent vase or a plume of ferns in a
bowl as my neighbor can with jack roses at
$5 a dozen in a cut glass epergne, the cost
of which would have kept a hungry family
in bread for a month. I can serve as palat-
able a company lunch of biscuits and honey
and foamy milk, with a bit of fruit and a
toss up of feathery cake or cream and have
fewer dishes for the girl to wash and fewer
bills for myself to pay, than the harassed
hostess does who employs a caterer and
uses a dozen plates and spoons and glasses
where one-quarter the number would suf-
fice. What rich woman is going to start
this business of simplifying? It needs
some one with wealth and prominent social
standing to pioneer the good work. Somebody told me not long ago of a wealthy
leader in society who kept up a distinct
establishment for her servants. She gave
them a parlor, a piano and a library. There
is a good place to begin to simplify. Go
back to old-fashioned methods of servant-
hire and give some of the rest of us who
have to work hard to keep a parlor and a
piano for ourselves, a chance to keep help.
Simplify all along the line, from the kitchen

to the guest chamber, and usher in a new
day.

Hospitality has been so utterly transposed
from its position among the virtues that it
has come to be something like the discord
occasioned by playing an F sharp in a C
scale. It is a source of constant irritation
both to nerves and sensibilities. We "expect" company, nowadays, but never are
blessed by our friends dropping in upon us
and taking things as they find them. Blessed
times when company meant a jollification
rather than a before-handed battle! When
the old carry-all rattled in at the side gate
and all the folks from the farm a dozen miles
away came over to spend the day. When
the girls took off their things and helped get
dinner. When grandma sat and knitted
worsted socks while she told us how to make
her kind of cream gravy to serve with crisp
fried pork. When the men folks went out
and looked at the crops that were safely
garnered in the barn, and coming back,
washed their hands and faces in water that
sparkled in a bright tin wash basin, and
dried them on homespun towels, clean and

sweet as grass. When we all sat down together to a dinner served in one course; ate dumplings shortened with cream rather than with cottolene, and drank coffee made without eggs and the color of an amber mouthpiece. When all turned to and helped do up the dishes, and sat down afterward and listened to the girls play duets on the melodeon or speak their exhibition pieces. Good old days! They will never come back again. They have been frightened away by shoddy style and an ultra civilization of progress.

* * * * *

Now, if we go visiting we are invited and we send acceptance on meaningless little scraps of conventional party paper. We know that our hostess is tiring herself out to make ready for us. We go, and are received at the door by a maid who helps us lay aside our wraps. And we dare not for our lives appear a minute before regulation time, as the breach of propriety perpetrated by appearing earlier than a quarter before 1 to a 1 o'clock dinner, is unforgivable. We wear regulation gowns and talk meaningless platitudes to uncongenial people

who are invited to meet us. We are confronted by a dinner which threatens a very
Banquo ghost of indigestion. We know
that enough labor has been put into its pro-
duction, and must still be carried on, in the
re-establishment of having in pantry and
kitchen, to run a mill that should supply a
hundred men. And we also know that the
husband of our host must work a little
harder for the time and pinch his under
forces a little tighter, to pay the bills that
come pouring in after a swell dinner in
uppertendom.

Oh for a new race of heroes! A band of
invincibles brave enough to face the world's
scorn and the sneers of pigmy revilers of all
things broad and best, until the new era of
right shall usurp the long-time tyranny of
might. A race of great hearts who shall be
strong enough, not alone to face lions and
dominate physical fear; who shall be heroic
not only in deeds of daring, such as charg-
ing mobs and scaling burning walls to save
property and life, but who shall have the
courage to maintain their convictions in the
most insignificant cause of good and
champion a new idea, however weak and un-
recognized it may be, in a world that is full

of pretense and pride, and the laughter of
fools!

I have often wondered if the fragrance of
a rose would be as delicious to us if the cen-
ser whence it emanated were less lovely; if,
instead of creamy-hued and dawn-tinted
petals, fine and soft as silk, the rose's cup
were made of the stiff, unyielding substance
of the thistle and the burr, or colored with
the neutral tints that mark the cabbage and
the cone.

But whenever such a doubt assails me, up
pops the little mignonette—that darling of
my heart, and carries the day for perfume vs.
beauty. Without a single line of grace, or
hue of splendor, that homely spiral of dingy
bloom appeals to the heart as no royal camelia throned upon its slender stalk has
ever dared to do.

You may enclose a blush-rose or a spray
of orange-blossom in a box, and send it to
the ends of the earth, and when the wrap-
pings are removed, although the flower is
discolored and dead, behold an odor that
fills the air like a spirit voice! Who thinks
then of the unsightly and withered petals,

or of the vanished beauty of the flower that was once so fair and comely? But pack the fairest camelia bud that ever lighted a summer dusk with its stainless glow, and send it with a message the wide world over, and when the box is opened, what have you? Simply a dead flower; and your message might as well seek utterance from the lips of the dead.

So you see it is the spirit which yields the only charm that endures in flowers. And what is true of roses is doubly true of girls. Mere graceful shape and splendid coloring are of small and worthless account, if there be no fragrance in the heart.

Now, girls, you are laughing, and you lay your fluffy heads of brown, and black and gold together, and say, "Oho! for Amber and her chestnut! We have heard all this before, and nothing is going to convince such wise young dames as we, that anything in this world compensates for the absence of beauty!" If you please, my dears, that is just what we are going to talk about, and if, when we are through, you tell me that you would choose to be an ever so perfect camelia rather than a dew-wet mignonette or a spray of homely lilac growing by a way-

side fence, then I will go to my room, and
send for a mason to wall me in! I don't care
to live another minute in a world where I
can't argue down hot-house and scentless
perfection with natural and heartsome
sweetness.

There is, and has been for many an un-
counted year, a false system in the world
whereby to grow our human roses, to estab-
lish the coronation of our bright young
queens. The mother begins with her two-
year-old daughter, and teaches her to be
strictly conventional. All the way up to
womanhood, in the hands of mother, nurse
and instructor, the little lass is taught to
do as others do, to keep step in the march
of the "great alike," and never dare to do a
thing, or think a thought, or speak a word
that can come under what weighs more
heavily than the sevenfold curse of Rome—
the ban of unconventionality. A young
girl is moved to speak a kindly word, or to
inconvenience herself to serve some shabby
stranger. Up go mother's, and nurse's, and
Dame Grundy's hands in horror! What!
go out of your way, my child, to show that
old woman a street, or carry an old man's
basket, or help a tired mother get her chil-

dren over a crowded crossing! Why, the
idea is absurdly out of the question. Such a
line of conduct will make people think you
queer, and far better be dead than that, in
the estimation of Vanity Fair, where your
life-booth is stationed.

By and by, grown a little older, and standing on the threshold of her first party, the
question of the low bodice first confronts the
young girl, and she intuitively shrinks from
the ordeal. But it takes but a little ridicule,
and a little flattery, to change the nature
that God meant to be a rose into a scentless,
dewless, blushless bit of millinery's perfection, no more to be compared to the blessed
Lord's intention than a bit of artificial muslin is to a bud in my far-away California
garden.

Then, dear girls, if you would be beautiful
with the beauty that strikes root in Paradise and will cast its blossoms in Heaven,
be natural. Be true to something within you,
higher than any mere conventional code or
worldly-wise mandate. If it is your natural
impulse to be courteous, and sympathetic,
and sweet, (and, blessed be God, it is the
natural bent of most girls,) don't let con-
formity's tricksters exchange your genuine

20

blossom for a mere shred of muslin, fashioned after ever so perfect a similitude of a
rose.　The birds of the air and the angels
in Heaven will never be fooled by an artificial blossom, however much dudes and so-
ciety-feather-heads may pretend to desire it.
Grow for God, not for the world.　Wear
your sweetness in your heart, rather than in
outside show.

There is nothing that will so absolutely il-
luminate a face as a fellowship in some other
body's good fortune than our own.　The
conventional smile that the artificial girl
wears, compared to the bonnie smile my
own true queen of girls wears, wherever I
find her—behind a shop-counter, in an
office, or on a clerk's stool—is as the illumination the sun makes on a June morning,
compared to the radiance cast by a single
pearl in the moonlight.　Both are fair and
alluring, perhaps, in their way, but the last
lacks warmth and soul.

Whatever service you may find it in your
way to render, then, my dears, be it loaning
a pin, measuring off a yard of ribbon, or saving a life, put a big pinch of heart in to season the transaction.

It is as easy to answer pleasantly the ques-

tion a stranger asks, although it may break
in upon your time, and seem to you to be of
little moment, as it is to respond grumpily,
and with uncalled-for reserve.

I can imagine the whole world coming
under the influence of sunshiny good-nature
and courtesy, as a strong man comes under
the influence of laughing gas, so that even
disagreeable and painful things that are
forced to happen lose their pain and their
sting.

Imagine a woman stepping on to a street
car, as many of us daily do, after a prolonged
chase through the mud. The first impulse
is to scold. But what good will that do?
All the hard things said can never undo the
happenings of a past minute. The conductor, born, in most cases, with a lifted heel
against mankind, is primed with a rude re-
tort, and the passengers are prepared to
stare, or laugh, or sneer, as the occasion may
require. But instead of a cross and haughty
protest, the injured woman is ready with a
good-natured laugh and a pleasant word.
How quickly the atmosphere changes! It
is as though a plume of lilac had swung
through the air. The conductor feels an
unwonted warmth in his heart, and the

woman leaves an impression of beauty behind her that will be recalled when perfect
features and a spotless complexion would be
forgotten. Who would not like to be remembered for a pleasant answer, or a gentle service rather than for a pretty nose or a
well modeled chin!

You want to live in this world, my dears,
as a spray of lilies lives in June. Every wind
that blows, be it great or small, through
your lives, should set an influence straying
like a perfume through the air. You won't
have to hunt out the breeze and the opportunity. All you have to do is to cultivate
the sweetness of your woman heart—occasions will be as recurring as the winds that
blow in summer.

Then continue to be more and more good-
natured and sympathetic and sweet-mannered, I beseech you, if the dear Lord made
you that way. Let no false idea of decorum,
or propriety, step in between you and the
performance of a spontaneous action of
kindness. Never fear that you can be too
good-natured and too amiable either in business or in social life. The same bright spon-
taneity of sympathy and good-fellowship
that makes home happy, will make office-life

and the space back of the shop counter bright also, if persevered in.

And if God did not give you a genial nature in the first place, cultivate it. Don't keep life a wilderness because you were not born to the direct inheritance of a rose-garden. You have a "fellowship with hearts to keep and cultivate," before you are fit for the companionship of angels.

Set to work, then, to plant slips in the desert before the time draws nigh when they shall find no warmth nor sunshine left in all the land to start them growing. Remember it is not always youth-time, any more than it is always May; and grafts and shoots that grow readily in spring will take no root in bleak November. Cultivate your smiles and your simple services of love now, and old age shall be but an afternoon trellis, hung deep with perfumed roses, as beautiful in the sunset glow as in the dawn.

How pleasant it is to meet people with whom everything goes just right. After coming in contact with the great parade of the dissatisfied it is like leaving a sawmill where iron teeth bite and sharp claws tear to while a happy hour by a sylvan brook that is full of sparkle and full of song.

I was once walking up the stairway of a suburban station with a mite of a woman as wee and sweet as a pea blossom. It was colder than an Arctic Christmas and the breath from our nostrils smote the air like white banners.

"Suppose we run in for a bit and warm our feet by the fire," said the small woman.

So we ran in, only to find the fire built in so lofty a stove that our ears barely touched the level of its radiating surface.

What did the little woman do when she discovered the impossibility of carrying out her plan? You or I perhaps would have exclaimed: "Bother take this old stove! Just like a railway corporation to make things uncomfortable for its patrons! The public ought to tear down these waiting-rooms as fast as they are built," etc. But my small friend said nothing of the kind. She merely looked around a bit and remarked:

"How nice and clean they keep these stations, don't they? The stove is pretty big, but I suppose it heats the place better."

"How about getting your feet warm?" I asked.

"Oh, it will take a little longer, but I guess we can spare the time. Too rapid heating of cold feet makes the worst sort of chilblains, anyway."

"You infinitesimal flick of sunshine," I wanted to say, "you ought to start the flowers growing wherever you pass!" I would rather have the disposition of that woman than wear court jewels and live in Windsor palace.

It is not beauty that makes a happy home, nor fine furniture, nor plenty of good food. It takes a sweet-natured and a comfort-distilling tongue every time to imbue four walls and a lot of upholstery with a soul. I have a mind to take a snap shot at a few homes I happen to know and see if my illustrations do not go far to prove my assertions.

* * * * *

First, there is the home of the Snapovers. They are a healthy, happy lot as you ever saw, but they have the fatal faculty of taking things hard. For instance, one of the girls sets a vase full of water on a handsome book. The vase holds violets and creates an atmosphere of Parmesian sunshine and sweetness all its own. By an accidental flip a few drops of water are spilled over upon the book. Straightway there is a veritable Sebastopol massacre of peace. The mother tears her hair and cries, "You have spoiled the book! Careless, careless girl that you are, behold what you have done!" The grandmother shakes like a withered leaf and offers religious consolation in allopathic doses.

"The dear Lord help us," she quavers, "in our hour of need! Your mother will die in one of these spells brought on by the thoughtless acts of her own offspring!"

"Ten dollars would not replace that work of art, ruined by an ungrateful child!" moans the father.

"You know I love you, mamma," weeps the daughter, "do you not? Believe me, I never meant to do this thing. Oh, it will kill me if you do not forgive me!" Meantime the hired girl comes in from the kitchen and complains that one of the children has broken a china cup. The tide of tears follows kitchenward and washes the emotional family thither on a foaming flood.

"How could you do so dreadful a thing?"

sobs the mother, while the afflicted father controls his emotions sufficiently to order the young culprit to bed.

Now these people have never known a big trouble all their lives. The father is prosperous; no disease has ever invaded the band, sudden death has not swooped down upon them like a meteor from the black bosom of night, and yet a more distressed and distressful household does not exist. To visit them is like loitering within the gates of a bombarded city. Everybody is keyed up to some great pitch of emotion perpetually. They live as they should live who await the summons of the high executioner from out a palace of delight. Of what avail the pictured walls and the tapestried doorways, when at any moment the silent messenger may summon them away to red-handed doom! Some day a real sorrow will invade the Snapover household, and there will be no reserve strength to meet it. The entire family will be in the condition of soldiers who, having used up their powder in spectacular fireworks, are helpless at the sounding of general alarm. Or like the little girl who cried "Wolf?" so often in play that when the genuine red-fanged monster of the forest bore down upon her nobody rallied to her relief because each one believed the outcry to be a false alarm. God pity the Snapovers when the actual bewilderment of an appalling calamity is upon them! They will be, I am afraid, like sheep that huddle together in the track of an advancing cyclone, or like the group of wind flowers that lie nearest the approaching wave of a prairie fire.

* * * * *

There is another household to which I am sometimes admitted as a guest. There are only three in the family, but the least one of all is a bald-headed tyrant of the Robespierrean type. His faintest blink is law, and the doubling of his tiny fist causes the heart of the boldest to quake. He is not two years old, but the supremacy of antique dynasties is heavy upon him. If he sleeps, the household, including the guest within the gates, suspend the breath and hush the footfall. If he wakes, there is nothing permitted to interfere with his wishes. Cares he to play horse? The father bends his patient back and canters to and fro like a steed of the desert. Does he sneeze? Every window is shut and adult cumberers of the

earth long for death. At the table, perhaps,
he evinces a sudden desire to walk upon the
viands. He plants one foot in the turnip,
and with a dimpled hand toys with the
mashed potato. He is removed from his
playground by force, only through fear that
the excitement will make him ill, not out
of regard for the sensibilities of the over-
fastidious guest. The children, of whom
this babe is a blooming type, always have a
tendency to over development of brain, and
for that reason need to be humored and deli-
cately handled. God knows, there is not sufficient brain development in the human race
at the best to discourage it in such a manner
as this. Rather an abnormal brain than the
torture of the home experience of a baby-
ridden family. Children are dear and sweet
in their way, but they should not be allowed
to run things with too free a hand. Gray-
headed men and women, even fathers and
mothers, to say nothing of superfluous and
silly guests, have a few rights, along with
the African and the alien, which a two-year-
old child should be taught to recognize and
respect.

* * * *

There is one more home I would like to

show you before I slip the slide and reverse
the picture. It is a country dwelling, and
all the beautiful gifts of nature surround it
like the wash of summer seas. There is a
crab-apple orchard at the side that puts
forth its frain of blossoms from year to
year, and later on yields spicy windfalls of
the prettiest fruit the sun shines on. A
vine drapes the gabled roof, and in spring
gives shelter to robins and bluebirds that
come and go beneath the shining of the mellow sun, or greet the dawn with flute-calls
and madrigals. Roses in companies, like
red-coated hussars, and ladies wearing pink
mantles and bonnets snow white and pinned
with dew, stand about that old-fashioned
homestead and curtsey all day in the mazes
of a stately minuet. Should not life be
happy passed in such a paradise? Within
the four walls, notwithstanding, there rests
the perpetual gloom of a shadow that never
lifts.

The male head of the family is a cynic, a
cold-blooded disbeliever in God, in virtue
and in love. He poisons with his malign influence every attribute of joy. He sneers
at everything pure and holy. His unfaith
blights the sweetest belief as the parasite

kills the vine. His mind is a charnel-house, and the effluvia of its own corruption blights the atmosphere about it. There can never be happiness where that man lives any more than there can be health near a sewer. How I should love to have the task given me to lift our friend with a pair of tongs and throw him over the fence, that such a home as he defiled might find the chance to achieve its own possibilities. With him removed from the circle, the will-crushed mother and the hypnotized children might begin to realize the life that God intended they should. There is no more chance for such as they to enjoy this beautiful world than there is for the leavening of bread with sour yeast, or the sounding of a harmony with a discordant string.

Taking things hard, then, selfishness and a perverted nature lie at the root of unhappiness in these thus hastily portrayed homes. For the first we have nothing but pity, mixed now and then with a little harmless ridicule. The poor unfortunates find no peace themselves and give nobody else any. They are always in a state of vibration, like the chords of a harp rudely stricken. They are stabbed twenty times a day by idle

words that were not meant to wound. They
are slighted and insulted and snubbed, according to their morbid fancy, when nobody
on earth ever intended to molest them. A
domestic tiff means hopeless disruption, an
ordinary headache is congestion of the
brain; an idle calamity, such as the deface-
ment of a book or the breaking of a bit of
crockery, means flagrant sin and humble
expiation. These people pass through life
like a lobster without its shell. Their skin
is thinner than rice paper and their heart is
pinned upon their sleeve. Every breeze
buffets them, every task drives them, every
vulture of care has its beak in their heart;
and I think at last the cool touch of the
death angel upon their fevered hearts
shall be like the soft hand of a mother upon
the childish brow that finds no rest from
pain's delirium. When God turns down the
lights and smooths the covers over these
poor restless ones perhaps they shall fall
asleep to awaken to the knowledge of what
a fuss they chose to make over trifles and
how foolish it all seems in the light of a new
consciousness.

For the selfishness that forgets all other
claims but what it owes to "big A" and "lit-

tle A," there is not so much to be said in commiseration. Selfishness is a prickly vice and hard to handle. It grows in every garden, and will never be uprooted from mortal soil.

If mothers who humor their children to the point of the unbearable would stop to consider that in so doing they do not create so much pleasure for the little ones as they awaken disgust in the hearts of all who come in contact with the darlings perhaps they would pursue a different course. There are very few parents who would not wish the highest good for those confided to their care. To know that the children who are so exceeding dear to them were generally referred to by outsiders as "little imps" and "holy terrors" might prove a barrier in the way of overindulgence. If nature had intended the baby to be paramount, nature would have installed the baby first and presented it with parents as an afterthought. The home that is ruled by unwisdom and immaturity must ever find its type in the stables (if such stables were possible) where the trainers are subservient to the colts and the jockeys are put through their paces at

the caprice of the entering two-year-olds of
the Derby.

I was sitting in a suburban train one night
not long ago awaiting the time to start. In
front of me sat a long-faced, erect gentleman of probably 65 or 70. His eye was keen
as a hawk's, and there was no sign about
him of waning power.

"It is nearly two years now," I heard a
voice say, "since Mary died."

"Two years the 5th of May."

"Ah, yes. Well, I suppose time is com-
mencing to rob the blow of its first sharpness?"

"If I looked upon her as dead," replied the
old gentleman quietly, "time could never
alleviate the sorrow, but to me she is not
dead; she is as much alive and even more
constantly with me now than ever before."

"You mean," suggested the other voice,
"that faith is so strong that you can locate
her, and behold her with your spiritual eyes,
in heaven."

"Not at all. Mary is not in heaven; she is
here on earth with me. Every evening I
read the paper to her and talk to her as I

used, the only difference being that she
makes no comments now. Every morning
I bid her good-bye and every evening I re-
peat the salutation. In ways that I can't ex-
plain she communicates with me, so that
but for the sound of her voice our commu-
nion is as perfect as it was for nearly forty
years."

"Am I to understand that you are going
over to the spiritualistic belief?" queried the
voice, while its owner peered a trifle nervously over a pair of silver spectacles at the
old gentleman.

"Understand what you please," was the
answer; "I tell you the simple truth; Mary
is with me, and but for that knowledge I
should be beside her in my grave. I am not
a believer in table-tippings nor materializa-
tion, but I am a believer in Mary, and know
that she is still with me."

God bless her! I hope Mary will never
leave him until she has permission to take
him along with her. I believe that about
the only consolation one gets in the supreme sorrow of death is out of the very
faith that makes us believe our dead linger
within the sound of our voices. The thought
of a far-away heaven where the baby I loved

21

or the friend I leaned upon are safely sheltered from sorrow and trouble is little comfort to me. I want them nearer still; so close that they can hear my cry and slip within my arms!

The last time. Did you ever stop to think of it? It is coming, perhaps it has already come, and you did not know it. You have gotten up for the last time from the chair where you have so long sat; you have closed the desk and slipped the key into the pocket whence your hand shall never take it again. You have read the last item of news from the familiar paper, and closed the covers of the last book you shall ever read on earth. You have looked for the last time into eyes that never failed to answer love with love; you have flashed the last message into the eyes of the enemy who has wronged you; you have looked your last at sunset sky and morning's roseate flush of dawn. For you the last cable car has swung around the corner and stopped to take you to your home for the last time. You have

turned out the lights and lain down in your
bed for the last time, and the stars that light
the midnight sky have flashed you their last
signal. You have taken your last journey,
written your last letter, eaten your last
meal, slept your last sleep. The story is
told, the play is ended, the lights are burning low, the music is hushed. Yet, most
potent of all in the significance of the
thought is the fact that your last opportunity for doing a deed of helpful kindness has
perhaps come. For the last time on earth
the chance confronts you to be gentle with
some one who has erred, to put out a strong
hand to some one who is weak, to say a
word in behalf of some one who is defenseless. Do not let love's opportunity go by
unchallenged, remembering always that it
may be the last you will ever know.